Just
What I
Needed

Kirsten S. Blacketer

Dedication

For Tim: You're just what I needed.

TABLE OF CONTENTS

Chapter One
Cyril

December 24, 1985

It's been a hell of a year.

Not that I'm complaining. Far from it. It's just…I've seen some crazy shit over the past twelve months. First, a girl from the future drops into my boss's lap, then I'm running all over town sticking my neck out for mafia busts, abuse allegations, and murder investigations. I'm not sure '86 can match the intensity of this year. Honestly, I'll be glad for a reprieve.

I turn up the heat and rest my elbow on the armrest. There's a line of cars in front of me, another line behind, my town car parked smack-dab in the middle. The Rolls is comfortable enough, but I can't ignore a pinch of jealousy at knowing my boss and his wife are enjoying a swanky holiday party in the Empire State Building.

Arthur Maxwell is the most prestigious architect in the city, and I've had the honor of being his driver for eleven years. Until this year, I've never thought of moving on, of trying my hand at something other than being a chauffeur. Don't get me wrong— it's a plush gig, and I get to do what I love, but it doesn't leave much time for anything else. Probably explains why I'm still single and haven't touched a wrench in ages.

With a sigh, I pull a pack of Doublemint from my pocket and stuff a stick in my mouth. My fingers tap the steering wheel in time with "More Than a Feeling" playing on the radio. Boston does their best to distract me, but the music doesn't touch my restlessness. I could go for a strong drink. Hell, even a cup of black coffee could do the trick.

Nodding along to the beat, I watch the entrance to the

building, hoping the boss will decide to call it a night early. The air is cold and crisp with a few scattered snowflakes drifting in front of the windshield, glinting in the streetlight. Shit. The snow isn't supposed to accumulate, but I don't like the combination of icy drizzle and snow. Makes a slushy mess and turns people into assholes behind the wheel. There's already a dusting of snow on the roads. I grimace when a man steps off the curb and nearly slides into the front of my car. Great.

I check the clock on the dash. Nine thirty. I cave to the boredom and pull out a paperback stashed in my glove compartment. Claude recommended it. One of Stephen King's novels, *The Shining*. I typically read science fiction, but I'm willing to give it a shot.

Four chapters later, I snap to attention as a couple approaches. Shit. I toss the book to the passenger seat and step out of the car, pulling my hat down so it won't blow away. By the time I round the front of the vehicle, Arthur and Kate have reached the curb.

"Sir. Ma'am." I acknowledge them with a smile and open the back door.

Arthur nods and helps his wife into the car.

"Thank you, Cyril," Kate says from the interior.

"Just doing my job." Once he takes a seat beside her, I close the door.

When I return to the driver's seat, my demeanor shifts to pure business, and without prompting, I head for Arthur's apartment. A few blocks down the street, I steal a glimpse in the rearview mirror. Kate's leaning against Arthur with her eyes closed. He has his arm protectively wrapped around her shoulder, keeping her close. He kisses her forehead.

My heart softens at the tender display. I redirect my attention to the traffic and ignore an ache in my chest. It's been too long. With my unpredictable, random hours, it's difficult for me to find anyone to invest in long-term. Romantically, I mean.

There've been women. Scores of them. But none with the right combination of smarts and sexy to last beyond a brief fling. Fun distractions, nothing more. Seeing Kate and Arthur together makes me long for something I never before realized I wanted.

Maybe one day, I can open a shop and have my own fleet of cars with a little garage to tinker with my own restoration project. If I had that, it would give me more time to find someone to share my life with. I shove the dream aside and focus on the road.

Arthur and I have spoken about it at length. He knows how much I want to start my own business, have my own space. I can't be his driver indefinitely. He agrees, even offered to be a silent investor in my business. But that's as far as it's gone. I'll talk to him about it after New Year's to see if he's serious about the project.

When I pull up outside their building, Arthur nudges Kate. "We're home."

"Already?" She yawns.

I chuckle. With the holiday traffic, the normally short drive took an hour. I put the car in park and step out to open her door, offering my hand when she moves to exit the car.

"Thank you, Cyril." She takes my hand to steady herself on the slick pavement. Her brow furrows. "Wait." She pats her pockets. "Is my clutch in the car?"

Arthur turns to check the back seat. "Nothing here."

"Damn. I must have left it."

"We can get it tomorrow." Arthur takes her by the elbow and leads her toward the entrance.

"I can stop and grab it on my way home, if you want." I curse myself the moment I say it because it will put me thirty minutes out of my way.

"No, it should be fine." She stops midstride and taps her lower lip. "Unless I left it on the observation deck…" Kate grips Arthur's arm. "I did. When you took me up, I left it on the lower ledge near the elevator."

Arthur's jaw clenches before he exhales in defeat. "Fine. I'll call someone to retrieve it."

"No need, sir. I'll get it."

"Are you sure, Cyril? I wouldn't want you to use personal time running an errand for me."

"It's fine." I force a smile. It's not like I have a family, or anything, to rush home to.

"Okay." Arthur leads Kate to the front door and turns. "See you at nine tomorrow morning."

"Yes, sir."

Once they close the door, I return to the car. Why did I offer to do this? I groan as I put the car into drive and pull away. The clock reads eleven fourteen. By the time I reach the Empire State Building, it'll be close to midnight.

The return trip takes less time. I park the car outside the building and pocket the keys. Ten minutes tops, then I'll be on my way home.

Inside, I slip past the night guard, talking on the phone. The elevator takes me to the observation deck. I pull my coat tighter around me, but the cold, wet wind still bites my face. I walk around for a few moments, searching the ledges near the elevator, until I spot it. Kate's clutch. I tuck it into my pocket and turn around.

The night sky spreads over the horizon, snow drifting lazily through the air. I step close to the railing, wanting the full immersive experience of the skyline stretched out before me. I inhale deeply and let the chill sink into my lungs to purge the restlessness for a moment.

What if this is as good as it gets?

Stuck in the mud, tires spinning.

No legacy. No family. Nothing to show but some memories and a few laughs. Have I run out of time to make something of myself? To leave my mark on the world?

Would anyone miss me if I were gone?

I shiver at the thought and force out an uncomfortable chuckle. Guess I'm more tired than I realized. I should go home and rest.

Spinning on my heel, I step toward the elevator, only to feel the slick ground give way under me. My hands fly out, searching for something, anything, to break my fall.

But there's nothing. I fall in slow motion for an eternity until the snow flecked night consumes my vision. Pain radiates through my head as I hit the ground.

Everything goes dark.

Warmth brushes my face. I open my eyes and blink into a sun-filled sky.

What the hell? With a groan, I carefully sit up and look around.

It all rushes back in a wave.

Observation deck. Empire State Building. I pat my pocket. Kate's clutch is still there. Shit, is it morning already? How the hell did I survive a night outside? I shake my head and climb to my feet.

The elevator opens behind me, and a group of people step onto the platform. They keep their distance as they move to the railing. I follow them, trying to make sense of my situation, when I see something.

Well, it's what I *don't see* that scrambles my brain.

"Where the hell is the World Trade Center?" I squint, searching the horizon for the tell-tale twins, standing tall at the base of Manhattan.

There's a single skyscraper in their place. What the hell?

A small group of people stare at me for a moment before moving to the far side of the platform. I ignore their stares and head for the elevator.

As the car descends, I rub my scalp. Maybe I hit my head harder than I thought and I'm still unconscious. I wince when I pinch my arm. Nope. Not asleep. My brain is sifting through confusing possibilities when the elevator reaches the ground floor.

I step into the lobby. When I pass the directory, I pause, searching the company names. Confusion fills me again when I reach the end of the list and haven't recognized any of them.

"Where's Arthur Maxwell?" I read the list again, but he's not there. Another name is in the space once occupied by my boss. Strange.

"Is everything okay, sir?" A guard comes alongside me.

"Yes, of course." I play it off, but inside, I'm in a full-blown panic. "Do you happen to have the paper?"

"The newspaper?" The guard gives me an odd look, like I've sprouted horns or a third eye.

"Yeah. Any paper."

"No, but I can pull it up for you." He takes a small rectangular device from his pocket, like something Spock would have on *Star Trek*. "*New York Times*," he says and the device dings.

"Here are some results for the *New York Times*." A mechanical voice emits from the device.

My mouth drops open. "Did that just respond to you?"

"Yeah. So?" He scoffs. "You sure you're okay?"

Am I okay? No. No, I am not.

"Can you just tell me what day it is?" I manage to ask the question, even though my throat feels like it's constricting, cutting off my airway.

"December 21." He turns the device, showing me a narrow screen with a photo of a cat eating noodles.

Then I see the time. And the date.

It's December 21…three days ago. But why does the year read *2022*?

My head spins. I brace myself against the wall.

"I gotta go."

Without a thought, I race through the lobby, out into the cool morning.

This can't be.

It can't be true.

I remember the stories Kate told us about what happened that fateful New Year's Day, but I didn't think it was actually true…that she traveled back in time.

And yet, I'm standing in the year 2022. Just last night it was 1985. My knees buckle, and I stumble to the nearest bench. Slumping into it, I hang my head in my hands.

The hustle and bustle of the city surrounds me. Pedestrians walking with intent. Horns blaring. Engines purring. Exhaust perfuming the air.

It all fades into the background as reality settles like a nail in a tire, leaving me deflated.

"Hey, buddy, got a dollar?" asks a man in a tattered green coat and threadbare stocking cap.

My hand reaches for my wallet, if only to ensure it's there. But it's not. I close my eyes and shake my head.

Of course. It's still in the Rolls. I never keep it in my pocket while driving.

"Sorry," I mutter to the old man.

He ambles down the street, disappearing in the crowd.

A breeze ruffles my hair, and I reach up to pull down my hat, only to find air. Shit. What happened to my hat? It probably got sucked into the void that is the space-time continuum.

I scoff. Too much science fiction. Damn you, Doc Brown.

I can't sit here all day wondering what the hell happened. I need to find Arthur and Kate. The Black Penny is close. Maybe Claude and Grant can help me.

Halfway down the block, I freeze midstride.

It's 2022. It's been thirty-seven years. What if they're...dead? Panic grabs me by the throat and chokes me. What if everything, every*one* I've ever known, is gone? Fuck.

I pull my coat tight around my throat again and push forward. Does it matter? There's not a damn thing I can do about it. Life moved on without me, and that's the painful fucking truth.

Even without me...the world kept spinning.

With every block, the confusion deepens as the reality of my situation settles deep in the pit of my gut. I'm barely aware of the people and noise around me. In thirty-odd years, the city and her people haven't changed much. Though the styles have evolved some. And everywhere I look, people are using little devices like the one the guard showed me. What the hell are they anyway? A tricorder? Some kind of handheld computer? As long as it's not some strange *Terminator* shit...oh God, there I go again.

Several blocks from the Black Penny, I turn right out of habit, heading home. My apartment—well, my former apartment—isn't far from the Hell's Kitchen hangout Arthur and his friends frequent. It sits above a two-bay garage run by a

Korean War veteran. Mac's Garage. He understands my need to have grease under my nails.

Is he gone?

Biting back my hesitation, I venture down the street leading straight to Mac's. To home. With every step, my heart pounds and my stomach lurches. I'm starving. I haven't eaten anything in….well, years. I feel like I'm going to puke.

I round the corner and the sign comes into view. I blink twice when I read it.

Cyril's Garage.

Wait. What happened to *Mac's* Garage? Why is my name on this building? I look up and down the quiet street. It's a small street and doesn't get much traffic. Today, I'm thankful for that. I stand in the middle of the road, staring at *my* name on the building where I lived thirty-seven years ago.

The sound of an air compressor echoes behind the large blue garage doors, drawing me closer. I pause outside the door, my hand resting on the knob. Muffled music hums through the air, vibrating the metal beneath my hand. When I push open the door, a familiar guitar solo lures me further inside. It's not a song I'm familiar with, but I know it's Aerosmith playing through the speakers. I'd recognize that screaming vocalist anywhere.

The clang of metal on concrete cuts through the music as the compressor cuts off. I venture deeper into the shop, taking in the familiar smell of grease and hydraulic fluid while noting the differences in the space. More organized, more colorful. More professional. Whoever owns this place knows their shit.

Then I see her—a 1974 green Dodge Dart Swinger.

I walk alongside the car, admiring the sleek lines. She's not finished, but I can see potential beneath the spotty rust and dinged rear quarter panel.

"Goddamn it." Another clang of metal strikes metal. "You miserable bitch. Why won't you cooperate?"

Is that a woman's voice? Curiosity pulls me around the car, and I see a curvy backside clad in denim bent over the front fender.

"Piece of shit! Just come off!" She jerks and pulls,

continuing to swear under her breath.

I peer over her shoulder, glimpsing the engine beneath the hood. I whistle low, noting the 360 V8. Not stock but definitely not overkill. Someone has some taste.

"Need a hand?" I ask on impulse.

She drops the tool in her hand and spins around, hitting her head on the hood of the car. "Motherfucker!" She grips her head with a grease-covered hand and hisses.

"Who the fuck are you?" Her deep blue eyes narrow at me. "Better yet, why the fuck are you in *my* shop?"

I suck in a breath. Shit. She's even more glorious than the car.

CHAPTER TWO
JESSICA

Damn it! I rub the aching spot on the back of my head and lean against the bumper, eyeing the man who disturbed my peaceful morning.

I should have checked the door to make sure it was locked. Anyone could walk in while I'm working, and I would never hear them. Real smooth. Cursing myself, I tighten my grip on the screwdriver in case I need to use it as a weapon.

My gaze skims the intruder. He's tall, dark, and distractingly handsome. Judging by the sharp suit and pristine wool jacket, he's not a vagrant wandering the winter streets, looking for a place to warm up.

I narrow my eyes and point the tool in his direction. "Again, who are you and why are you in my shop?" I grit my teeth, irritated. "We're closed."

"Door was open." He shrugs in the general direction of the entrance.

"We're still closed."

His eyes sparkle with amusement. "Is that how you treat customers?"

"Are you a customer?"

"Depends on whether this is your typical customer service."

I roll my eyes. "Listen. We're closed for Christmas. All our services are booked for the holiday. But thanks for coming in. Don't let the door hit you on the way out."

I turn back to the engine, ignoring the way his perusal of my shop and my car makes me acutely aware of his presence.

He doesn't move as I reach down to adjust the carburetor.

"What are you doing?"

"Working." I ignore him and focus on my task.

"Why are you doing it the hard way?"

I sigh with exasperation, then glare at him. "What? You wrench?"

"A little." He shoves his hands in his pockets and shrugs. "Been a while though."

With a scoff, I turn back to the engine and continue my adjustments. Why does everyone assume I don't know my way around cars? Seriously. I've been doing this since I was eight. I don't need to be mansplained.

He steps closer, leaning over the bumper. There's six inches between us. I try to ignore him and focus on the carburetor. His warmth drifts to me, carrying the spicy, subtle aromas of cologne and leather. I refuse to react to the way it tickles my nose and weaves through my brain, short circuits sparking in its wake. My grip tightens on the screwdriver again, and I twist harder.

The tool gives under my hand and slips free, clanging against the compartment. My wrist nicks a sharp clamp edge near the radiator, and I curse as a spasm of pain radiates up my arm.

"Damn it." I jerk my hand free and pull a rag from my pocket to wrap around the cut. Biting back tears of frustration, I lean against the car and close my eyes.

"Let me see."

His soft voice pulls me from my pissy solitude. I open my eyes, and he's holding out his hand.

"It's just a scratch. I got it." The warmth seeping through the rag tells me it's more than just a scratch. Shit.

He huffs, like he can see through my tough act, and takes my hand. The moment his fingertips brush mine, the protest dies on my lips. I bite my tongue and watch in silence as he removes the dirty rag to examine the cut.

"Not deep enough for stitches, but we'll have to clean it up." He tosses the dirty rag aside and wraps a clean one around the wound, putting pressure on it. Where the hell did he get it? Must have grabbed it from the box on the shelf while I was bitching myself out for carelessness.

"I can take care of it." I jerk my hand out of his and head for the bathroom.

Inside, I close the door and lean against it. What the hell? Who is this guy? And why does he leave me off-kilter? I push the questions aside and wash the wound. Thank God I keep a first aid kit here. Once it's clean and wrapped in a sterilized bandage, I take a minute to compose myself.

I snort when I look in a small mirror on the door to find grease smeared across my forehead and cheek. How attractive. I shake myself. Why do I care? I'm working. I get dirty when I work. Any mechanic would know that. I use the damp rag to wipe the grease off.

Looks like I'm done for now. Just need to take the car out for a test drive before I make more adjustments.

Now to deal with the elephant in the room. I *wish* he were an elephant and not a tempting distraction with soulful eyes and a sinful smile. Nope, not going there.

Find out who he is and what he wants, then show him the door. Simple.

When I step back into the garage, I stop at the sight before me. He's bent over the front of my Swinger, the distinctive *click* and *tink* of metal against metal sounding from beneath the hood. What the hell is he doing to my car?

By the time I reach his side, he's pulled back and is wiping his hands on a rag.

I open my mouth to tell him he's a presumptuous ass for touching my baby.

"I made a little adjustment for you. Should start easier next time."

"That's bold, to barge into someone's garage and touch their goddamned car without permission." I glower at him before looking at the place he's indicating. He managed to adjust it just like I wanted, but I wouldn't be sure until I started the car. How the hell did he get the damn thing to cooperate?

Doesn't matter. I'm still irritated.

"Didn't mean to overstep. Just looked like you needed a helping hand." He smiles, and two identical dimples appear.

I brace my hand against the car. If he'd been handsome before, he was smoldering hot now. That alone pushes me from mildly irritated to pissed.

"All right, who the hell are you? Did my dad send you?" I cross my arms.

My dad's been on my case to find a partner to expand the business for years. But I'm not interested. This garage is *mine*. I've worked too damn hard to let some jackass come in here and steal it from me. It would be just like Dad to invite someone to come in as partner without my approval. Agitation itches beneath my skin.

"No one sent me." His brows draw together in confusion. "Is this your place?"

"Yes." Pride fills me as I look around the shop. "Why?"

"Your name is Cyril?"

That wicked smile curves his lips, and I'm momentarily distracted by the casual charm oozing off him.

"No." I shake my head and curse Dad, yet again, for being adamant about keeping the name he chose when he bought it years ago.

"Do I have to beg for it?"

His question leaves me stunned. My breath catches, and his eyes—green now that I see them up close—sparkle with mischief. "Beg…for what?"

"Your name." His voice, deep and even, feels like a distraction.

I bite my lip. Do I really want to tell him my name? There's something about him that feels off, but we've been alone together long enough for him to have hurt me if he really wanted to.

I exhale sharply in defeat. "Jessica."

"Jessica," he repeats, and I'm not turned off by the way my name rolls off his lips. "Pretty name."

"Thanks." I unruffle myself and prop a hand on my hip. "You gonna tell me your name and what the hell you want?"

He sets the rag aside and grins. "I'm Cyril. I'm looking for an old friend."

"Cyril?" Disbelief punches me in the chest, stealing the air in my lungs before laughter replaces it. I double over and slap my thigh. "That's a good one. Did my dad put you up to this?" I grumble under my breath, "I'm gonna strangle that old grump."

The humor in his eyes dims. "Who's your father?"

"That's it. He's gone too far. This is ridiculous." I pull my iPhone out of my back pocket. His gaze lingers on the device, and I swear there's a mix of curiosity and panic in his shifting facial expression. I ignore it and press the button. "Siri, call Dad."

"Who's Siri?" he mutters to himself more than to me.

The line rings, and I put the phone to my ear. "Pick up, Dad." My frown deepens with each unanswered ring. Finally, his voicemail kicks in. Screw it. I hang up.

Then I notice the time. It's nine thirty. Mom and Dad had an appointment this morning, uptown. They won't be back until noon. Shit. I glance at my wary companion.

His face is pale, his eyes fixed on a spot of oil on the concrete. My heart constricts at the way he looks like a lost puppy in the middle of Central Park. Damn it. None of this makes sense. Dad's up to something…but I'll be damned if I know what it is.

"Who's your father?" he asks again, his voice softer this time.

"Like you don't know."

"Please."

Whoever this guy is, he's not my problem…and yet, that one word echoes through the shop, fading into the music coming through the speakers. It breaks my resolve to stay detached.

"Arthur Maxwell."

His eyes pinch shut, and he sucks in a deep breath. When he turns away on his heel, I can almost feel the tension radiating from his dark form. He rakes both hands over his head, threading his fingers through his hair. After a few moments, he heads for the exit.

This guy is off his rocker. I should be happy he's leaving, but guilt claws at my gut. Damn it.

"Hey," I shout, jogging across the concrete to catch him before he reaches the door. I grab his sleeve and pull him to a stop. "Wanna grab something to eat? There's a place around the corner. My treat."

His shoulders relax. I brace myself as he turns. The strong jaw I admired earlier is clenched tight. Gone are the dimples, replaced with a somber demeanor.

"Thanks, but I don't want to take up any more of your time."

"Look, I'm sorry I was a dick earlier. Let me make it up to you." My hand tightens on his sleeve. "Please."

God, how desperate do I sound? Anything to quell the pressing guilt for being a complete asshole to a stranger.

When his green eyes meet mine, I smile, trying to show a little repentance.

One dimple appears as he responds. "Food sounds good." The second dimple appears. "I'm starving."

"Good. Great." I release his sleeve, suddenly overwhelmed with warmth. "I'll grab my coat and lock up."

He waits by the door while I run to the office for my things. I switch off the lights, leaving only one light on near the front door. He's leaning against the wall when I reach him. I finish tugging on my coat.

With one arm, he pushes open the door. "After you."

"Thanks." I step out onto the sidewalk and turn to lock the door after he comes alongside me.

There's a chill in the air. Feels like snow. I pull my jacket tighter and turn right, toward the diner. He falls into step beside me, and there's something weird about this whole encounter.

We walk in silence, a million questions burning a hole in my head. I bite them back, uncertain I want the answers. I shouldn't get involved. This guy isn't my problem.

And yet...

I study his profile. Strong and sharp, angular and regal. Why does he look familiar?

Something twists deep in my chest before breaking loose and nestling in my brain, tugging at a forgotten memory.

It's probably my guilty coincidence.

I just hope Dad's not trying to pull a fast one on me.

CHAPTER THREE
CYRIL

The diner apparently hasn't changed in thirty some years—chrome and glass, neon *Open* sign glowing in the window. Dirty, caked snow litters the sidewalk as we approach the door. Instinctively, I step around her, reach for the handle, and open it.

"After you." I gesture with a sweep of my arm, as I've done for years as her father's driver.

Her incredulous look sticks with me, even as she steps into the warm restaurant. I follow behind.

The aroma of fried, greasy food assails me. My stomach grumbles, pleading for attention. It's like I haven't eaten in years.

Wait…that's more true than I want to admit. As the reality of my situation sinks in, I square my shoulders and really take in my surroundings.

While the diner is largely the same, it's older, faded in spots. There are no familiar faces behind the counter. The restaurant is busy, but the conversation is muted. Then I see why. Most people are focused on the small devices in their hands rather than the people sitting across from them. It's not true in all the cases, but enough to make it noticeable. Sad and strange.

A waitress appears, wearing casual clothing instead of the blue-and-white uniform I'm used to. "How many?"

"Two," Jessica responds before I can.

The waitress snatches two menus and leads us to a booth tucked into a corner near the window.

"Sam will be right over." With a nod, she turns to leave.

"Wow," I mutter under my breath. Things have certainly changed. What happened to service with a smile?

"What?" Jessica asks, glancing up from the open menu in

her hand.

"Nothing." I shake my head and skim the words on the menu. Then I see the prices. "Holy shit."

"Something wrong?" She folds the menu and sets it aside.

"When did breakfast get so expensive?" I rub my forehead trying to suppress an oncoming headache.

She scoffs. "It's gotten worse over the last two years. Trust me. The pandemic jacked up everything."

"The...pandemic?"

I bite my tongue at her exasperated look.

"Yeah, let's not talk about it, okay?"

"Okay." I have no idea what she's talking about, but I admit I'm curious. There will be time to catch up on the events of the past thirty-seven years later. Especially if I can get one of those distracting handheld devices—phones? computers?—everyone seems to have.

A waitress appears, her hair a bright neon pink. Sam, I assume. "What can I get ya?"

Jessica gives her order first. Coffee with cream, two eggs over easy, hashbrowns, and sausage. It sounds delicious.

"I'll have the same," I say when Sam looks at me. I hand her my menu. "Thanks."

After she retreats, Jessica leans back and pins me with those gorgeous blue eyes. Her dark hair is still pulled up in a messy heap on top of her head, but the grease stains are gone. Bummer. They were kind of sexy. Everything about her is sexy.

But she's Arthur's daughter.

The thought instantly sobers me. I clear my throat and wish I had coffee to distract my hands and my mouth. Shit.

"So...you gonna tell me how you know my dad?"

I clear my throat with a cough, covering my mouth. Sam appears with our coffee and creamer. I use the interruption to my advantage. While I pour cream into my steaming coffee, my mind spins. What the hell do I tell her? I can't tell her the truth. She'll never believe it.

As I scramble for a realistic response, she watches me, echoing my actions before taking a sip of her coffee. Her soft groan of satisfaction shoots through me, leaving goosebumps along my arms. Damn it.

I drink my coffee too fast and burn my tongue. Today is really not my day, is it?

"Well…" I set the cup aside. "It's complicated."

"How is it complicated? You met him *somewhere*."

"He's an old friend. We met years ago." I hope she'll buy the vague response.

"Where?" She leans forward, resting her elbows on the table. The curve of her T-shirt dips low, and I catch a teasing glimpse of cleavage.

I look out the window to clear my head before finally meeting her intense gaze. "The Empire State Building."

"Dad hasn't worked there in thirty years." She scoffs. "How old are you?"

"Thirty-nine." At least, that's how old I *look*. Oh damn, this is complicated. I ignore the physics of time travel and the complications I'm compounding onto the space-time continuum. I pray I'm not irrevocably fucking something up in the universe or causing a rift in our timeline.

"You met him when you were young?" Her brows scrunch together as she digs deeper. "How?"

"I admired his work. Wanted to meet him." I sip my coffee. "He inspired me to work hard." I'm not lying, but if she asks more questions, I may have to spin some pretty creative tales.

"How old are you?" I ask, turning the tables, praying it will distract her from her current inquisition.

"Thirty-two. Why?"

"How long have you been turning wrenches?"

"Since I was eight." She points a finger at me. "Stop turning this around to me. I'm not stupid. I know what you're trying to do."

"What am I trying to do?"

"Distract me." Jessica glowers. "It won't work."

"I'm not trying to distract you," I lie with a placating smile. "I'm genuinely curious about how a gorgeous woman finds herself fixing vintage cars in a garage."

"It's *my* garage." Her eyes narrow. "Are you sure Dad didn't send you?"

"Nope. I was taking a walk and saw my name in lights. Had to check it out."

A small smile cracks her lips. "That's another thing. Your name. It's not common."

"No, it's not, but I'm partial to it."

"What are the odds of you passing by a garage with your name on it?"

"Pretty slim." My eyes widen. "Maybe it's a sign."

"A sign of what?"

"Fate."

Jessica scoffs. "You're as crazy as Dad."

"What do you mean?" I crave information about Arthur and Kate. Jessica is my only connection to them. If I can somehow convince her to take me to them, I can explain everything. They'll believe me. They're the only people who will understand.

"Dad always talked about fate bringing him and Mom together." Jessica rolls her eyes. "Sentimental ramblings of an old man."

Fate did bring them together. I saw it with my own two eyes. I remember the day like it was yesterday, vivid and fresh in my mind, how horror filled me when I saw Arthur exit the Empire State Building with an unconscious woman in his arms.

Who was I to question my employer? I bit my tongue and drove him home, even though my conscience told me to take her to an emergency room. Arthur convinced me he had it under control. It was the only time in my tenure as his driver when I questioned his judgment. In the end, he was right. It worked out.

Even though it had been difficult for me to believe Kate was from the future, there was always something about her that set her apart from everyone around. Something special. The way she spoke, her mannerisms. Hell, even her humor set her apart.

I miss them, Kate and Arthur. They were more than my employers; they were my family, my friends. Everything I had, I owed to their kindness. Did they mourn my loss? Questions burn, but I can't ask them. I need to see Arthur.

"I wouldn't be so quick to mock fate." My tone is soft between us. The spot between my ribs above my heart aches at the loss I've suffered…a gaping black hole of time I'll never get back.

"You sound just like him." She shakes her head.

The food arrives, giving us a reprieve. I pick up my fork and eat, not tasting the food I shovel into my mouth. I'm starving, but this hunger is for much more than sustenance. I quietly steal glances at Jessica between bites.

She devours her food with enthusiasm. Must have worked up an appetite arguing with me. I smile to myself and finish my breakfast.

I'm not sure if she trusts me, or even if she believes a word that has come out of my mouth, but I don't care. I'm at her mercy, even if she doesn't realize it. She's the easiest way to connect me to the only people who will understand the insane situation I'm in.

I'll survive, regardless of what happens, but right now, I need an anchor. Something to ground me. To hold me steady. To give me purpose and direction.

As I finish my eggs, I catch Jessica's eye. She offers the first sincere smile I've seen so far. Something inside my chest twists, rips open, and sinks to the pit of my stomach in a warm fizzle of resignation.

I thought Arthur and Kate could offer some solutions to my complicated situation. Maybe I've already found the answer.

Maybe Jessica is just what I need.

Thanks, Fate.

CHAPTER FOUR

JESSICA

There's something weird about this guy. Not in a *I'm afraid he's a serial killer and I'll never see my family again* way. No, it's subtle…an undercurrent of electricity pulsing through my body. Familiarity nags at my brain, but I've never met him before. I know I haven't. I would remember a guy this hot.

He runs his fingers through his thick, dark hair and looks out the window. The way his eyes scan the world beyond the glass makes me think he's searching for something. For someone? He appeared out of the blue this morning—maybe he's wandering. Lost.

Damn it. I don't need this right now. Dad's put a lot of stress on me lately with his persistent suggestions to find a partner and expand the garage. We have a healthy clientele and a steady schedule that covers the bills. Why this sudden need to expand?

I mean, he and Mom are in their seventies now. They won't be around forever, but I don't need them to take care of me. I haven't needed it for a long time. After my divorce, I took control of my life and poured my heart and soul into the garage. And it's flourishing.

Is there room for expansion? Maybe. But why push when I'm content where I am? Besides, expansion means taking on a partner, and that's the *last* thing I want right now.

When the waitress returns with the check, I hand her my card.

"Thanks for breakfast," Cyril says, fidgeting with the edge of his placemat.

My heart softens at his tone. "You're welcome." A ding vibrates my phone in my pocket. I pull it out and read the text from Mom. *Dad and I are on our way home. Is something wrong?*

I quickly type out a reply. *Got a surprise visitor this morning. He wants to speak to Dad. I'm bringing him over.*

Mom replies with a thumbs-up emoji.

I shake my head and put the phone away.

"Everything okay?" He looks even more lost with that confused expression.

"Yeah, we're good." I take my card back from the waitress and sign the receipt, slapping a cash tip on top. "Ready to go?"

"I guess." He stands and pulls on his coat.

Once we're on the sidewalk, he tucks his hands in his pockets and falls into step beside me. Strange how comfortable I feel in his presence after our unusual meeting this morning.

We cover the short distance to the garage, and I unlock the door. The Swinger gleams beneath the shop lights. I grab the keys off a hook in the office.

"Let's go for a drive." I head to the driver's seat.

His brow arches when I open the Swinger's door. "You sure she's roadworthy?"

"Get in," I snarl. She's more than roadworthy. I had her running fine before. There are just a few kinks I want to work out with the carburetor. Once I get those fixed, I can finally take her to the body shop for a fresh coat of paint.

I look at him when he slides into the passenger seat. A teasing smile lingers on his lips, betraying a glimpse of those dimples. He's fucking with me. I jam my finger on the button to open the garage door. It slides up behind me, and I fire up the Swinger.

She purrs like a kitten. Nothing else sounds so good. Years of hard work and scrounging for parts has finally paid off. I slide my hand over the steering wheel and put her in reverse.

After slowly backing out, I close the garage door behind us. Once I'm sure it's down and locked, I shift into gear. She crawls forward with confidence. Most of the snow has melted from the roads, and the slick spots are dry. Should be clear all the way to Eighty-First Street.

I ease her down the narrow road and out onto the main

street into traffic.

"Might be faster if you take Park Ave." He checks his watch. "We're past rush hour."

"I think I know the fastest way to get to my parents' house." I hazard a side-eye before refocusing on the traffic around me.

"Sorry." He throws his hands up. "Force of habit."

Silence envelops us. I turn on the radio and let a classic rock station fill the void. Bon Jovi drifts from the speakers, and I sing along under my breath as I weave through cars, around a truck parked on the curb with flashers on. Just another day in paradise.

Cyril stares out the window, searching the sidewalks and buildings. His eyes widen, but his lips remain pressed firmly together.

I feel bad for him. I really do. He seems confused sometimes. Disoriented. But his eyes are clear, his tone steady. He's not on drugs, though he might need meds. Somehow, I don't think that's the case though. He just looks…out of place. Uncomfortable. It's strange.

Hopefully, Dad can help him. I know I can't. I have too much other shit on my plate to take care of this lost little puppy, no matter how attractive he is.

Forty-five minutes later, I pull up outside the brownstone on Eighty-First. Normally, I have to fight for parking, but there's a spot waiting today. I might want to play the lottery. I put the Swinger in park, turn off the engine, and pocket the key.

"Where are we?" he asks, stepping onto the sidewalk. A woman walks by with two toddlers, one clasped in each hand.

"Home," I reply, gesturing to the stone building, the only home I've ever known. It still looks exactly the same as when I was a kid.

"Your parents live here?" He turns to face the house. "Since when?"

"Late eighties, I think." I lock the car and come alongside him. "Come on, they're waiting for us."

I take the steps two at a time, careful not to slip on black ice. Cyril follows with measured steps.

I unlock the door and step inside, hanging my jacket and

scarf on a hook by the door. "Hang up your coat here."

Dad has the gas fireplace on, warming the living room. I smile as memories surround me. Such a great home to grow up in.

Cyril stops at the doorway to take in the room. "Nice place."

"Thanks." I wave toward the couch. "Have a seat. I'll get my parents. I hear them upstairs." The floor creaks overhead, affirming my statement. "I'll be right back. Make yourself at home."

With a nod, Cyril wanders into the living room.

I make my way up the stairs. They knew I was coming over. Where are they?

At the top of the stairs, I knock on the first bedroom door. "Mom? Dad? You here?"

The door swings open. Mom blinks at me. Her hair is completely white, and she styles it to neatly frame her careworn, lined face. When did she get so old? I hug her.

"What's this about a visitor?" she asks, her eyes wide and sparkling. "I had to put new batteries in my hearing aids. Oh, how exciting."

"Where's Dad?" I glance behind her.

"I'm here. What's all the fuss?" Dad lumbers into view, leaning heavily on a cane. His gray hair is neatly combed, and his blue eyes flash.

"There's someone downstairs to see you."

"Who is it?"

"I don't know him. He showed up at the garage this morning claiming he knows you."

Dad taps his cane on the floor. "Does he have a name?"

"He says it's Cyril."

Mom gasps and turns to Dad. They share a long, knowing look. Tears prick at Mom's eyes. Dad takes her hand and pats it between his. Neither speaks.

I feel like I'm missing something important.

"What's going on?" I ask hesitantly, afraid the moment might burst like a soap bubble.

"Come on." Dad pulls Mom out of the bedroom.

I stare after my parents as they slowly make their way down the stairs. These two should live on the first floor, but nothing I say will convince them to change. They're set in their ways. I sigh and follow dutifully behind.

At least now I'll get some answers. I hope.

CHAPTER FIVE
CYRIL

The moment Jessica leaves the room, I steady myself against the back of the chair.

This is surreal.

I pinch my eyes closed and hope I'm dreaming. I'll wake up and find myself in 1985, running late to pick up Kate and Arthur. My gaze skims the furniture, worn in a lived-in way. This house has seen nothing but love and life for the past thirty-some years.

Jealousy rears its head, and I'm buffeted with the reminder of all the time I've lost. I manage to shake the thought free when I spy photographs hanging on the wall. As I drift closer, my heart warms at Kate's familiar smile and Arthur's halfhearted effort at one.

Some of the images feel like yesterday. Kate and Arthur at the Black Penny. Their wedding day at the top of the Empire State Building. A lovely shot of them in Rome, standing by the Trevi Fountain. I continue looking. In one photo, I can make out the grainy shape of my car in the background with me standing beside it, waiting. My face is impossible to see, but it's me. Always in the background. Always waiting.

I wander around the room, taking in moments I missed, moments held within the photographs. By the time I reach the mantel, they're family snapshots. Kate with her arms around three children, Arthur standing behind them. The photo captures pure joy. It lures me in and holds me captive.

As I study their faces, I can see the older two children, a boy and a girl, inherited Arthur's dark coloring and brilliant eyes. The youngest looks like Kate with her wild curls and bright, mischievous smile.

Jessica.

I laugh. It has to be her. The girl in the photo has the same spark in her eye. The same defiant stance I saw this morning when I stumbled into her workspace.

With every photograph, I find myself searching for her, trying to identify each person. Kate and Arthur poured their hearts and souls into their children, that much is evident in the images surrounding me. They seized each moment and made memories to last a lifetime.

Memories of a time I'll never experience.

I step back and put my hands in my pockets. Regret and disappointment creep in, wrapping around any hope of returning to the past. Kate was never able to get back to her time. She embraced the moment, the opportunity fate placed before her. She took a chance. Can I really do the same?

Uncertainty sinks like a brick in the pit of my stomach. It's barely been half a day and I'm already floundering.

I missed so much. Kate and Arthur. The crew from the Black Penny. They were my family. My circle. When I disappeared, what happened to them? Did they miss me?

I see the memories documented in film and shake my head. No. They went on. They embraced the moment and lived life to the fullest.

Life went on without me. It's selfish to think the world stopped revolving simply because I wasn't there.

Where was I? That's the question. One I'll never get an answer to, but it nags at me regardless.

"Cyril?" Arthur's voice, as familiar as my own, echoes behind me.

I turn, and Kate's gasp fills the air.

Arthur and Kate are old and gray. I was ready for it, thanks to the pictures around the room, but nothing could have prepared me for the shock of seeing them in person. It was just yesterday when they were young, vibrant, full of hope and life, brimming with love for each other.

"Arthur." I meet his gaze before shifting my own to his wife. "Kate."

She leans against her husband, one hand covering her

mouth. A sob catches in her throat.

"Cyril." She crosses the room, reaching for me. I take her hands, feeling her wrinkles against my fingertips. My heart breaks at the passage of time and the mark it left on my friends.

"You look stunning, Kate." I grin at her.

She scoffs and wraps her arms around me, hugging me tight. "We were so worried about you."

I fold her into my embrace, unable to find words. She's so delicate, so frail. Goddamn it. I can't stop the tears pooling in my eyes. When I look up, Arthur steps closer.

"I'm glad you found us." Arthur claps his hand on my shoulder. The force of it startles me. For a man in his seventies, I wouldn't expect such a firm grip…but this is Arthur, so I'm not sure why I'm surprised by his strength.

"I wouldn't have found you if it weren't for your daughter." My attention shifts to the woman in the doorway.

Her stiff posture relaxes with my acknowledgment, and she drops her arms to her sides. "You weren't lying." The firm set of her lips softens to a hesitant smile, and she steps into the room. "But it doesn't explain anything. I still have questions."

"Oh yes. So do I." Kate releases me and guides me to sit beside her on the sofa.

Arthur settles into a recliner by the arched entryway, and Jessica leans against his chair, watching the scene with a skeptical eye.

"Where to start?" I laugh, trying to ease the tension in the room.

Kate takes my hand in hers and pats it the way my grandma used to when I was young. "Would you like something to drink? Coffee? Tea? Whiskey?"

"Nothing, thank you. I just had breakfast."

"What happened, Cyril?" Arthur's question cuts to the heart of the matter. "When you never showed up for work, we assumed the worst."

"Until I suggested you were transported like I was," Kate adds, nudging me with her elbow. Her luminous eyes search my face. I can see the woman she was all those years ago reflected in their depths.

"I returned to retrieve your purse…" I release her hand and reach into my jacket pocket. Her clutch is still there, tucked in the deep recesses of the fabric. I pull it out and hand it to her.

She gasps and runs her fingers over the beaded material. Tears fill her eyes. "I never should have sent you." Her voice cracks. "This is my fault."

"No, Kate. It isn't your fault." I pull her against me. "You couldn't have known this would happen."

"I knew that place had…has…this strange ability to transport people through time." She sniffs. "For years, I pushed it from my mind, thinking it was a freak accident. A coincidence. That what happened to me was a one-in-a million occurrence."

"Here I am." I smile and stroke her age-worn cheek. "Guess that makes us special, doesn't it?" At her smile, hope sparks in my chest. "Do you think we're the only two people to travel through time? We should start a support group, see if others come."

When she laughs, my heart bursts.

"So you got caught in the time portal, or whatever it is, and ended up here?" Arthur asks, stroking his jaw. "Why *now*?"

My gaze shifts from him to Jessica, leaning against the side of his recliner. Her green eyes burn through me. "I have no idea," I reply, keeping my focus firmly on his daughter.

"How did you meet Jessica?" Kate asks.

"When I woke at the top of the Empire State Building, I realized I wasn't in 1985 anymore."

"The towers," Kate says knowingly. "That was my first clue too."

"What happened to them?" The question slips out before I can stop it from derailing the conversation.

"Terrorists flew planes into them," Jessica replies. "September 11, 2001."

"Changed more than the skyline, that's for sure," Arthur mumbles.

"Dad." Jessica nudges his shoulder. "Don't start."

He throws his hands up but continues muttering under his

breath.

My curiosity is piqued, but I force myself to stay on track. There's plenty of time to find out what I missed over the last thirty-seven years. From the sound of it, I missed a lot more than family vacations.

"Once I realized the date, I went to the only place I had any connection to."

"The garage." Arthur leans back, his hands steepled, fingertips tapping.

I nod, keeping Jessica in the corner of my vision, watching her reaction. I can't help it. It's like I need her to believe me, to understand this is the truth, no matter how crazy it sounds.

"You went inside?" Arthur's expression remains impassive.

"I did." I swallow and sneak a full peek at Jessica.

Her jaw clenches.

"I found your daughter working on the Swinger." I clear my throat. "Obviously, I didn't know she was your daughter, but when she asked if I knew her father…well, the missing pieces fell into place."

"I see."

"I need to know something." I chew the inside of my cheek, unsure how to ask, and decide to be blunt. "Rob and Marcy…are they…"

Kate takes my hand. "They're alive. Living upstate."

"And the crew from the Black Penny?" I look at Arthur and hold my breath.

"Still around. Retired, of course, but we see them all once a month when we get together for breakfast." Arthur's head wavers for a moment. "Grant had a heart attack a few months ago, but he's doing better after surgery."

Relief floods my body, and I sag back against the sofa. "Good to hear."

"Claude's daughter runs the Penny now." Arthur chuckles. "She's a piece of work. Don't cross her."

I blink twice before it registers. Of course they all have families. Children and grandchildren. I nod and swallow the lump in my throat.

"This is strange." I gesture to myself. "I haven't changed, but everything I know has."

"It does take some time to adapt," Kate assures me. "But you're a quick study. You'll figure it out."

What if I don't want to adapt? The question rises in my mind like a flashing neon sign. I quickly dismiss it. I don't have a choice. There's no going back to 1985. I'm stuck here. I'd better make the best of it before I get crushed.

"I'm glad you're still here." I look between Kate and Arthur before my gaze lingers on Jessica for a moment. "I don't know what I would have done without you."

Jessica's brow furrows. I redirect my attention to her father.

"You don't need a driver anymore, do you?" I ask hopefully.

"No, but I'm sure we can find something to keep you busy." Arthur exchanges a long look with Kate.

I shift at its intensity. Am I missing something?

"First, we need to get you caught up." She takes my hand and stands, leading me to the mantel with all the photographs. "These are our children. Sandra, Matthew, and Jessica." As she goes down the photographs, I take in every detail. She tells me where the photo was taken along with the story behind each one.

Slowly, she fills me in on thirty-seven years of Maxwell family adventure. Arthur fills in details when she asks for his input. Jessica remains silent, as still as a statue, poised beside her father. Watching. Listening. Waiting.

I can't help but feel she's taking my measure, weighing me against the stories her parents have told her…if they told her anything at all about me.

Curiosity burns hot as her cold stare follows where her mother leads me. She disappears, leaving me alone with Kate and Arthur. When she returns, she's bearing a tray of steaming coffee mugs.

She hands me a plain green cup. Why do I suspect she'd poison me if she had the opportunity?

Even though Kate and Arthur have welcomed me with open arms, my presence has the opposite effect on their daughter.

I have the distinct impression Jessica hates me, and I'm determined to unravel the mystery as to why.

CHAPTER SIX
JESSICA

My head is spinning.

When Mom dives into the story of our trip to the Grand Canyon, I decide I need a break. Escaping to the kitchen, I take a few moments of peace to rearrange my thoughts.

So this guy isn't crazy. He knew Dad, worked for Dad years ago. I remember hearing stories about his driver, but I never paid attention to his name or what happened to him. My parents are great storytellers, how was I to know *these* stories were true?

Agitated, I measure the coffee grounds into the antiquated Mr. Coffee and fill it with distilled water. Nothing about this makes sense. And yet, Mom always told us the story of how she and Dad met. How she traveled through time and wound up on the top of the Empire State Building.

It was just a bedtime story, right? Now I'm not so sure.

This guy, though. I don't trust him any further than I can throw him. He magically shows up, and he's Dad's long-lost driver? I scoff as I pull the mugs from a cabinet by the sink. Maybe he's trying to pull a fast one on Mom and Dad? He could be a swindler.

But then, how the hell would he know Uncle Rob and Aunt Marcy? How would he know the crew from the Black Penny?

Something about this doesn't add up.

It can't be a coincidence that this stranger's name is Cyril. Hell, I've never even met anyone with that name. I've always just associated it with the garage because that was its name when I was born in 1990. I wasn't even around when Dad bought the garage, but he always told me he did so for a friend.

What are the freaking odds that *friend* shows up on our doorstep? If I were a betting woman, I'd put money down it's impossible.

But the laughter in the living room tells me otherwise.

The fresh scent of brewed coffee drifts around me as I fill four mugs and place them on a tray. I add a container of cream to the tray before lifting it. Takes me back to the two weeks I tried my hand at waitressing in college but ended up dumping two plates of spaghetti on some guy's head. I definitely wasn't cut out for food service. With careful, measured steps, I return to the living room and place the tray on the coffee table.

Mom has moved on to stories of my nieces and nephews. I ignore the way Cyril's gaze follows me, handing him the green mug and picking up my own. It's hard to keep my expression impassive. I don't want to upset Mom and Dad, but this whole situation is hard to swallow.

"Sounds like you've had a great life." Cyril sips his coffee.

"We have," Mom says with a whimsical sigh. "We are very fortunate."

"It's good to finally have some closure though." Dad sets his mug aside. "We searched for you for months. Years. We never gave up hope that one day you'd return."

"You couldn't possibly know that." Cyril scoffs.

"You're right, but I held out hope it would all come full circle." My father leans back in his chair. Today, he looks every year of his age.

My heart aches when I realize I don't have much time left with my parents. I shove the thought aside and finish my drink.

"What will you do now?" Mom asks, her eyes shining with interest.

"Well…honestly, I don't know. Should I go to the DMV and renew my license? They'll never believe my age."

Dad waves his hand. "Don't worry about that. We had the same issue with Kate. There are ways around it."

"Not legal ones, Dad," I mutter under my breath. He shakes his head at me, but I persist. "You can't just expect him to pick up where he left off. It's been thirty-seven years."

"You're right." Dad strokes his jaw. "Things have certainly changed."

"I don't want to be a burden," Cyril assures us, breaking into the conversation. "I'll figure things out. It'll just take time, a little trial and error."

"It will be easier if you have someone to walk you through it."

I can feel Dad's attention shift to me, and I pinch my eyes closed. *Please don't. Don't drag me into this mess. I have my own shit.*

"Jessica could give you a hand. She's a whiz with computers. These millennials have knack for technology."

"Millennials?" Cyril asks.

"People born between the early eighties and the year 2000." I sigh at the explanation. "There's a whole generation thing now. Trust me, you're better off not knowing."

"What would I be?"

"Boomer." I mutter the word. "Can we move on?" I turn to Dad. "I have a lot going on at the garage. I can't do anything else right now."

"That's the genius to my plan." Dad's eyes sparkle, and I grit my teeth, bracing for it. "He can give you a hand at the garage."

"Dad…" I sputter. "I don't know…" Anger and frustration bubble inside me but I bite back the words, knowing how much they'll affect my parents. Instead, I just listen, helpless and raging inside.

"Cyril knows his way around cars. He was my driver for years, and he helped in the garage when it belonged to Mac. You'll make a great team." Dad grins like he's found the solution to all of life's problems.

"Team?" I bite the word and long to spit it in the trash.

"Yeah, partners. Bring him into the business, teach him the ropes. With both of you behind the wheel, you should be able to expand within the next year."

There it is. Even though my dad didn't send Cyril this morning, it's come full circle. The one thing I don't want has been dropped into my lap—a boomer dinosaur plunged into the twenty-first century. And I'm expected to play babysitter. Fan-fucking-tastic. What's next? Will Dad give him the garage and cut me out completely? The thought turns my blood to ice before it transforms to molten lava. My hand flexes against the couch, gripping the seam.

"Partners?" I shake my head and count to ten. "Dad, maybe we should talk about this…"

"There's nothing to talk about. Cyril's back." Dad beams. "He's practically family. The least we can do is help him get his bearings."

"But where is he going to live?"

"At the garage. Hell, his stuff is still in the attic."

I can't even bring myself to look at Cyril. None of this is his fault, not directly, but that doesn't mean I have to take it lying down.

"Dad, where am *I* supposed to live?"

"There's enough room for the two of you. You'll make it work. At least until he gets his feet under him."

"Sir, I…" Cyril tries to interject, but Dad cuts him off.

"It's settled then."

"Nothing is settled, Dad." I turn on him. "I've lived there for fifteen years. I've worked there since I was a kid. That garage is my life. It's my…"

"It's *my* investment." Dad fixes me with a stern look. "I hold the deed to the building and a controlling stake the business."

I bite my lip, stifling curses I want to hurl into the room. This isn't fair. I've worked so fucking hard to get to this point. Dad can't seriously give it all to some guy he hasn't seen in nearly forty years?

There's no way I can break. Not here. Not now.

Somehow, I manage to smother the tears and push up from the couch. I can't sit here another minute. Not when everything I've worked for hangs by a thread…a thread held by my father.

I won't do it. There's no way I will stand aside and let Dad give my dream to someone else.

"Jessica." Mom's voice follows me as I leave the room.

I keep walking, unable to bear the pressure of being in that room for a moment longer. I need to breathe.

At the back of the house, I pause near the side door in the

kitchen. Panic overwhelms me, and the dam holding back my tears finally snaps. I swipe them away with the back of my hand.

This isn't fair. It's not *his* family. It's not *his* dream. *He* doesn't deserve to have it all handed to him on a silver platter.

And I shouldn't be expected to bend over backward to help my replacement.

Fuck. Is Dad trying to replace me? He's always been supportive of me, of my vision for the garage, for the business. Why now? Why *him*?

Inside my chest, my heart is being shredded, like an old tire beating on the highway. I thought I was stronger than this, but it seems today is full of disappointments.

I stare into the small garden beyond the back door. It's barren and cold. Hopeless, just like me.

If I want to keep the garage, I'll have to abide by my father's wishes.

I've never detested his obstinate nature more than I do at this moment.

I hate this.

CHAPTER SEVEN
CYRIL

"It's *my* investment," Arthur says to Jessica, his expression stern. "I hold the deed to the building and a controlling stake in the business."

My body tenses at his statement. It wasn't my intention to stir up trouble. I didn't want to demand anything from Arthur or Kate. I just wanted to see my friends again, to make sure they were alive and well. To make sure my absence hadn't, in some way, left a scar.

While I'm confident they missed me, I'm glad it didn't stop them from living their lives. But fate has a funny sense of humor, dropping me into this decade unprepared and ill-equipped to deal with what I will find. What are the odds the first person I encounter, other than the guard, would be the daughter of my employer?

Jessica's eyes flash with unharnessed fury. If it were anyone else saying those words, I'm sure she'd rip them apart. But because it's her father, she bites her tongue and stuffs it down. Her body stiffens as she stands, her hands clenched in fists.

When she exits the room without another word, Arthur's stern expression falters. He closes his eyes and covers his face.

"Jessica!" Kate rushes after her daughter as fast as her elderly legs can carry her, casting a silent apology over her shoulder before leaving the room.

Several minutes pass, and I struggle with indecision. Part of me wants to leave. I can find my way on my own. I can make it work. There are jobs out there. Places to live. I don't want to burden anyone. I won't be a burden. It's clear Jessica feels strongly about the garage and her role there. I would never come between her and her father. I'd rather live on the street and beg for change.

"I'm sorry about that." Arthur's gruff voice cuts through the pensive silence.

"There's nothing to apologize for, sir." I fold my hands in my lap.

Arthur chuckles. "I think we're beyond 'sir,' don't you?"

"No, sir." I laugh softly. "But if you want me to call you something else, I will."

"Arthur. Please. We're beyond an employer-employee relationship now."

"If I take you up on your offer…technically, we're not." I gently broach the topic, knowing he offered but unsure how to negotiate around Jessica's unwillingness to take me on as a partner.

"She'll come around," he says, as if reading my thoughts.

"I don't want her to do something she doesn't want to do."

"Forcing a woman to do *any*thing is a surefire way to get nowhere fast." He sighs and nods. "Nearly forty years of marriage has taught me that."

"Then don't ask her to take this on. Don't make it her responsibility to teach me how to live in this time. I can figure it out on my own."

Arthur leans forward, groaning with the movement. He meets my gaze, and all I can see in his eyes is worry. "I know you can. No matter what, I'll help you get back on your feet. You did your job better than any driver I've ever had…and after you, I went through a lot of them. They could never live up to your standard."

"Thank you, sir." My heart warms at his kind words. "It was an honor to work for you."

"You were…*are* part of this family." He nods firmly. "Whatever you need, it's yours."

"I—"

"The garage is yours."

His words choke me. "What?"

"The garage. It's yours, been yours since I bought it in December 1985."

"You…" The implication of his words sinks into my brain. "You mean…Cyril's Garage is…"

"It's yours." He smiles at my obvious confusion. He can't be serious? But he is.

"You just…" I hazard a glance at the doorway and lower my voice. "But you told Jessica you are the owner."

"I know what I said." Arthur waves his hand. "But I bought that place for you. An investment in your business. I was going to transfer the deed to you on Christmas Day, but you disappeared."

"Sir, I can't…"

Words completely fail me. His belief in my abilities, his kindness, his generosity. It overwhelms me with emotions.

Then I remember the passion in Jessica's eyes at the mention of the garage. "Thank you. But don't you think circumstances have changed?"

"Have they?" Arthur leans on the arm of the recliner.

"Your daughter…"

"I'll take care of Jessica. She won't suffer. That I can promise you."

"But why would you demand she take me on as a partner and not tell her the truth?"

His blue eyes still hold the intense gleam I remember. Time hasn't stolen his fire and determination. I can see exactly where Jessica got her quick tongue and sharp mind.

"What are you up to?"

"Who says I'm up to anything?" Arthur reclines in his chair and kicks his feet up.

I study his smug expression, then it hits me. He's setting me up with his daughter. Forcing us to work together in the hopes something will happen. My God. He's playing matchmaker. I can't call him out on it. I'm not against spending time with Jessica to see if there's any chemistry between us that could spark a relationship. But there's no guarantee this plan will work. It could fall apart in spectacular fashion, and there would be a lot of carnage. This situation is strange, but what if I'm misreading the whole thing? I need to figure out his motive before I let this go further.

"You're playing with dynamite, putting her in a position like this."

"You think I don't know my daughter?" He scoffs. "She was my shadow for years. I thought she would be an architect like her dad, but when she showed more interest in cars than buildings…well, I couldn't deny her. She's my baby."

"All the more reason for me to *not* get involved." I clear my throat. "Whatever beef she's got with you is your problem. Don't put me in the middle of it."

"You're already in the middle of it, Cyril." His eyes gloss over, unfocused, as if he's lost in thought. "I won't be around forever."

"Sir?"

"I want to be sure she's taken care of—not financially, that's covered, and God knows, she can take care of things herself." The worry returns, making him pale. "She deserves to be happy. With someone who understands her."

"We barely know each other." But with one look at his face, I concede defeat. He won't listen to reason. "I can make sure she's taken care of, but there's no guarantee anything will happen between us."

"Do you know why I kept the garage? Why I kept your things in storage?" He reminisces with a grin. "Everyone thought I was crazy. Called me foolish. Even Kate."

I shake my head, unsure what to say. It seems his mind is made up, and everyone knows you don't argue with an old man. Nothing scares them anymore.

"I knew you'd be back." He presses his hand to his chest. "Every time I thought about selling, about giving up, something here stopped me."

"Sounds crazy."

"That's what Kate said." He chuckles. "But after finding her, after experiencing what we've experienced, I knew I had to continue on faith it would work out."

"There's no dissuading you from this, is there?"

"No."

"Just to be clear…" I pause, searching for the right words. "You want us to become partners in order to push us together as a couple?"

"Yes."

"This is weird."

"I know. Trust me. It was weird to see Kate as a baby while she stood right next to me." He shakes his head. "It was weird knowing the woman I was marrying hadn't even been born yet. Knowing there was an age gap a mile wide between us, even though we were technically peers if anyone saw us together."

"Okay, okay. I get your point." My brain hurts at the way he says it. "So you're okay with your daughter and me being in a romantic relationship?"

His smile fades. "I don't need the details, Cyril. Just make this work."

My mind replays my first meeting with Jessica. I was so busy lusting after the car, I'd barely registered a mechanic hiding on the other side. But the moment I saw her will be forever emblazoned on my brain.

"I don't think it will be a problem, sir."

"You're already half-smitten with her, aren't you?" His knowing smile spreads wider.

"Doesn't matter if I am. She hates me."

"She'll come around."

"And if she doesn't?"

"She will." Arthur shrugs. "All she needs is a little nudge."

"This is more like throwing her into the deep end of the pool."

"She can swim. I taught her."

The parallel isn't lost on me. Jessica is more than capable of taking care of a business and herself. I'm positive she learned everything from her old man. I just don't want to be on the receiving end of her fire.

"There's always a choice, Cyril."

"A choice?"

"If it doesn't work, you can walk away." He taps his fingers on the leather arm of the chair. "Start over. I'll help." His voice wavers. "Just give her a chance. That's all I ask."

I'm on my feet and across the room before he can react. When I offer my hand, he takes it.

"I'll do my best, sir."

Hope radiates from him as he pumps my hand. "I know you will."

The shuffle of feet in the hall pulls us from the moment. He releases my hand, and I gather the coffee mugs to put them on the tray.

I'm not sure how I'll be able to live up to his expectations. Or how he expects me to convince Jessica I'm not a monster who's taken the form of her father's former employee, sent to devour everyone. Maybe I've watched too many science fiction movies.

I take a deep breath. How the hell do you work with someone who trusts you about as far as they can throw you?

CHAPTER EIGHT
JESSICA

"Honey?" Mom's voice echoes behind me.

My body tenses, and I brace for the conversation. I saw the way Mom acted around Cyril, how she is with Dad. She always tries to smooth things over, to quell the conflict before it has a chance to start. She's good at it too.

But I won't relinquish the betrayal and fear racing through me. My hard work, my dream—they're too important to just throw aside like yesterday's newspaper.

She rests her hand on my shoulder. I close my eyes, unable to face her.

"Come on, let's sit in the kitchen." She tugs my sleeve.

There's no avoiding this. Begrudgingly, I follow my mother into the kitchen. She sets a tin of Christmas cookies on the table.

I snatch a snickerdoodle off the top before slumping into a chair opposite her. They're my favorite, and she knows it. Plying me with cookies is never a good sign. I stare at the cabinet while I nibble the sugary treat.

Mom grabs an oatmeal raisin cookie and sits patiently. Finally, she speaks. "What's going on in your head, honey?"

I sigh. "I don't want this."

"Want what?"

"I don't want to be in charge of bringing a fossil into the twenty-first century, Mom." I set the half-eaten cookie on the table.

"Cyril is hardly a fossil, sweetheart."

"I have enough to deal with. I don't need one more thing on my plate." I grind my teeth at the thought of him being in my space all the time. "I don't have the patience to coddle someone."

"He's not a child. You don't need to coddle him." She wipes her hand on a napkin. "I understand."

"Dad doesn't." I cross my arms. "He'll push until I snap, and then all hell will break loose."

"I think your father is worried about you running the business alone." Her voice is gentle, but I hear it in her tone. She agrees with Dad. "Maybe you should give it a try. A partner might not be a bad thing."

"I don't need a partner butting into *my* business, telling me how I should run things."

"I doubt he'll do that."

"You don't know what he'll do. That's the point." I throw my hands up. "You expect me to just take your word about this guy? You'll gladly give him a job and free access to whatever he wants. You're too trusting."

"He's never given us any reason not to trust him." Mom's brow furrows. "I know it's difficult to understand, but I've been where he is—lost in a time that isn't mine, without direction or resources."

I roll my eyes and mumble under my breath, *Here we go again.*

"He worked for your father for years without complaint." She studies my face. "The least we can do is help him get on his feet."

"By giving him *my* garage?"

"Ah. There it is."

"There *what* is?" I frown.

"The truth." She reaches over to take my hand. The warmth of her skin soothes my agitation, but I'm still pissed at this whole situation. "You think your father is going to give the garage to Cyril."

"It's *his* business. He can do what he wants." I throw Dad's words at her.

"You're right. It is. But do you really think your father would do something like that without discussing it with you first?" She squeezes my hand.

"I don't know. Would he? He doesn't seem to care what I want right now."

"That's not true."

"It is. He's not even willing to listen to me." I gesture toward the front of the house with a wave of my hand. "When Dad gets it into his head to do something, nothing I say, nothing I do will change his mind."

"Maybe you should give it a try." Mom cocks her head, her mismatched eyes carefully studying me. "What's the worst that could happen?"

"Dad giving away everything I've worked for." Passion laces my words. "I've busted my ass for years to get the garage to where it is now. I'll be damned if a stranger will come in and wreck all my hard work."

"No one is trying to ruin anything, honey."

"Yes, they are." My voice rises in pitch as my agitation grows. "That garage is my haven. My baby. I've dumped all my time and energy into it. It's *mine*."

"You've worked hard—no one is saying you haven't—but you need help. At least give this partnership a try and see if it works out."

"And when it doesn't? Then what happens?"

"We'll cross that bridge when we get to it," Mom says diplomatically.

"I don't want to cross that bridge later. I want to address it now, before this whole mess implodes." I push my hair away from my face.

"Honey, don't you think you're being dramatic?"

"No. I'm not. This is my *life*, Mom. It's not a fad or a hobby." I take a deep breath. "I don't want a complete stranger coming in and telling me how to run my shop."

"I don't think Cyril will do that."

"Mom, he told me I was fixing a carburetor the 'hard way' before he even knew my name."

Mom chuckles. "That's men, sweetheart."

"That's exactly what I mean. Say I agree to this madness…he starts telling me all the things I'm doing the 'hard way.' He'll think his way is the only way to do anything, and I'll end up in prison for murder."

"Jessica." Mom's laugh echoes through the kitchen. "You really are my daughter with that flair for the dramatic."

"I'm serious, Mom. I won't let some guy from 1985 muscle his way into my life to mansplain things I've been doing for twenty years. I'll kill him."

"He's not the only man you've had to work with over the years, and you've yet to be charged with assault, let alone murder."

"There's always a first time," I grumble.

"It's not easy working with someone you don't know, but personal growth isn't supposed to be painless."

"You're dead set on this, aren't you?"

"I agree with your father."

"Why is Dad so determined to make this partnership happen?"

Mom shifts in her chair and exhales. "Before Cyril disappeared, he showed your father a business proposal."

"A business proposal for what?"

"A car service and garage."

Realization flashes like a light flickering to life in my mind. "Dad bought the garage as an investment, and Cyril was supposed to run it."

"Exactly."

"But then he disappeared, and Dad held onto the business in case Cyril returned."

Mom nods, a relieved smile on her lips.

"Now that he's here, Dad's trying to make good on his promise." My anger and frustration take a backseat to crushing disappointment. "So I've been keeping this business alive for years, just in case Cyril showed up?"

"No, honey. Your father let you run the business because he saw how much you love working on cars. How good you are at it."

"But now Cyril's back, I'm expendable."

"That's not true at all, and you know it."

I stare out the window, avoiding her gaze.

"Jessica, your father and I love you. We want you to be

successful and happy." Mom rests a hand on mine, and I fight tears.

"Don't make me do this."

"You're the only one who *can* do this." Mom's eyes are brimming with tears too. "No one will understand his situation the way you do."

She's right. I hate that she's right. I don't have a mean bone in my body, but every cell is screaming at the injustice of what they're asking me to do. I pinch my eyes closed.

"Give it a few months. Help him get settled. If it doesn't work, we'll figure something else out."

I turn to face her. "Promise?"

"I promise."

Relief filters through me. Even though I'm not committed to this whole arrangement, knowing there's a light at the end of the tunnel makes it more manageable. I still have some stipulations before I agree to anything, but I nod.

Mom beams with joy. "Wonderful. Now, let's go back to the living room. I'm sure you'll want to discuss details with your father and Cyril."

She knows me so well. I wrap her in my arms and inhale. "Thank you, Mom."

"I love you, sweetheart." Her voice quavers. "Things will work out. They always do."

"I know." Uncertainty lingers in my mind, but I shake it off.

I can do this. I can show Dad and Cyril I don't need anyone holding my hand. I'm thirty-two, and I run a successful business on my own. The last thing I need is a man telling me how to do my job.

Mom squeezes me tight one more time and heads back to the living room.

I take a few deep, cleansing breaths, readying myself for the next round with my father. He's about to find out how well I paid attention to his lessons in negotiation. I'm his daughter, and I inherited more than just his blue eyes. Stubborn is our middle name.

CHAPTER NINE
CYRIL

Jessica walks into the room, and uncertainty punches me square in the chest. I'm not sure I can do this. She deserves to know her father's plan, but there's no way I can tell her. Or that she'll believe me.

No, I'm the enemy. I can tell from the way she glowers at me.

How the hell am I supposed to get her to work with me? From the daggers she's glaring in my direction, I'm pretty sure she'd shove me in front of the first train we come across or drown me in the Hudson if given the chance.

Learning to navigate the future with limited information and no resources was going to be hard enough, but having a grudging partner will make this ten times more difficult. I'm a quick study, and while it's hard to wrap my head around the fact that I just skipped nearly forty years of history and technological advancement, I'm not intimidated by it.

I grew up on science fiction. Nothing they have today will throw me for a loop. I guarantee it.

"Well?" Arthur asks Jessica, pulling me from my thoughts.

"Well, what?" She sniffs and ignores me even though we're standing only five feet apart.

"Are you willing to take Cyril on as a partner, show him the ropes?"

She turns to face me, and I'm stunned by how vivid blue her eyes are. Like a clear summer sky.

"I'll do it, but"—she holds up a hand to stop me from speaking—"I have a few conditions."

"Okay."

Jessica gapes. "Don't you want to hear what they are?"

"Do I get to counter?" I ask.

"No." Her brow arches, almost in challenge.

"Then no, I don't need to hear what they are." I shrug. "It doesn't matter. I'm not exactly in a position to negotiate."

She blinks twice and turns to her father. "He gets two months. If it doesn't work, we part ways, and I continue running the shop like I have for the last ten years."

Arthur's jaw tenses and his eyes narrow. "Six months."

"Three."

"Four," he counters.

I watch the volley between them. It's like I'm not even in the room. These two would make a formidable team. I can see why Arthur put her in charge of the garage. It's also apparent he needs someone to balance her. A strong temperament can stall business without someone to push them in unexpected ways.

"That's my final offer, Jessica. Take it or leave it."

"Fine, but he's not staying in my apartment."

"It's big enough for both of you." Arthur cocks his head. "Besides, all his stuff is already there. No reason to hunt down another place and move everything."

"He'll be moving in four months anyway," Jessica mutters under her breath.

I can't help but laugh. She side-eyes me, and it dies in my throat. With a cough, I look at Kate, who's wearing a knowing grin.

"Fine." Jessica throws her hands up. "Is that all?"

"For now." Arthur rises slowly to his feet, arching his back. "I'll call you if there's anything else."

Jessica stands and hugs her father.

"I love you, Jessie."

"Love you too, Dad." She squeezes him before stepping to the side and hugging Kate.

Keeping back, I watch the interaction, warm affection filling me. Kate and Arthur are my family, especially Arthur. When I had nothing but the clothes on my back and a hotwire kit in my pocket, he took a chance on me. Gave me a job and an opportunity to make something of myself.

Jessica steps into the hallway, leaving me to say goodbye to her parents.

Kate wraps her arms around me. "Take care of yourself, Cyril. You know where to find us if you need anything."

"Thanks. I will." I kiss the top of her head.

Arthur's expression is guarded, but I see a glimmer in his eyes, reminding me of our conversation. I offer my hand. He pulls me into a hug.

"Take care of her. She'll come around." His gruff whisper is low enough to stay between only us.

I nod when we pull apart, and he claps a hand on my shoulder. "Good to have you back."

"Thank you, sir."

Jessica's waiting for me in a small alcove by the front door, already wearing her jacket. I grab mine from the hook and pull it on. I reach behind her, and her eyes widen when I step into her space to grab the doorknob. She steps aside when I open the door.

"After you."

Her lips press into a thin line as she spins and heads into the cold December air. I admire the way she stomps down the front steps.

"Good luck," Kate says behind me. "You're gonna need it."

"Right." I give her a little salute and follow Jessica to the car.

We reach the dark green Swinger, and she pulls the keys from her pocket as she rounds the front end.

"Mind if I drive?" I ask, knowing I'm, yet again, tempting fate by even voicing the question.

"You want to drive *my* car?" She scoffs. "Want me to have Dad give you the deed to the shop while we're at it?"

Guilt settles around my shoulders, but I shrug it off. Nope. Not going there. "Just want to give her a spin, see how she handles."

Her hand rests on the driver's side door. I can almost see the gears spinning in her mind. She closes her eyes and sighs, her shoulders briefly slumping. When she looks up, I hold my breath.

A slight breeze catches her curly hair, and all I can see is the perfect blend of her parents in her features. Arthur's bright blue eyes and stubborn streak. Kate's delicate bone structure, curly hair, and dangerous curves. If someone had told me I'd be standing in the future, admiring my boss's daughter, I'd have thought they were smoking the good shit. How can this be real?

"Fine." She walks around the car and hands me the keys. "But if you hurt my baby, I'll snap your spine. Got it?"

"Got it." I clench the keys in my fist and head for the driver's seat.

I glance up at the brownstone before I climb into the car. Sure enough, Kate and Arthur stand at the picture window, watching with matching grins. I wave and climb into the Swinger.

Let's see how well she does with a master behind the wheel.

Kate grinds her teeth when I start the car but doesn't say anything.

"I got this." With a smirk, I put her in gear and pull out onto the street. "Trust me."

Chapter Ten
Jessica

What the hell was I thinking, letting him drive my car?

I grip the armrest on the door as he maneuvers away from the curb. The roads are clear, but it still makes me nervous. He says he's a competent driver—and if he drove for Dad for years, he must be—but it does nothing to ease the knot occupying my stomach right now.

He eases the throttle up, taking to the streets with ease. Confidence ebbs through him as he rests his arm on the door and controls the wheel with one hand. His gaze flicks from the street to the mirrors and back again.

I should be disturbed by how good he looks sitting in the driver's seat of *my* car. Instead, I'm disturbed by a fluttering where my heart beats. Confidence is sexy, but when a man knows his way around a car, things can only go one of two ways—either I'm completely turned off by his arrogance, or I'm drawn to him. Right now, it's the latter.

Nope. We're gonna stop that right now. Dad might have slapped us together as partners for the next four months, but that's it. That will be the end of this whole…whatever's going on here.

It's bad enough I have this hurdle to overcome, but to have to babysit this dinosaur, attractive or not, only serves to agitate me further. Fuck. I don't like complications. And this is most certainly a massive complication. I should have known when I got up this morning and everything was going smoothly, that something bad would happen. It always goes sideways just when I'm starting to get my feet back underneath me.

It's been three months since I heard from Justin. Bastard dumped me in July when I refused to fix his piece-of-shit car for free. Dude, I'm not a charity organization. I have clients who pay me very well for my expertise. Just because I'm dating someone, it doesn't give him first dibs on my time or my knowledge. You wait, or you pay. He didn't like that, so he called off a three-year relationship. Buh-bye. Don't let the door hit your ass on the way out.

I should have learned from my failed one-year marriage at twenty-three, but I blame that on being young and dumb, smitten with lust.

"Mind if I turn on the radio?" Cyril asks, reaching for the knob.

"Knock your socks off." I nod to the stereo. "Driver picks the tunes, passenger shuts his cakehole."

His laugh curls through me like tendrils of warmth after drinking hot tea.

"Never heard it put like that, but I like it." He turns on the radio and cringes at the blast of music coming from the speakers.

"What's wrong?" I ask as he searches through stations.

"Is this music?" He looks physically pained with each passing song. He stops, and his expression relaxes at the sound of "Moving in Stereo" by the Cars. "Finally."

"A classic rock station?" I laugh, running my hand through my hair. "Of course you like the old stuff."

"It's not old stuff to me." He taps the steering wheel as we slow to a stop at a light. "I guess more than music has changed in thirty-seven years."

"Yeah, you got that right." I shift at the time that has elapsed for him. I'm nearly thirty-three, and I feel like an old lady some days. "So what do you want to know about the future?"

"Have they made another *Star Wars* movie?"

"Are you seriously asking me about *Star Wars* right now?" I blink at him. "Of all the things in the world that have changed, that's your first question?"

"I figure I need to know the most important information first." He glances at me, his eyes sparkling. "So...did they?"

"Yes."

"Really?" His excitement grows. "Come on, don't leave me

hanging."

"They made three prequels in the early 2000s, and then some sequels in the mid-2010s."

"Yes!" He cheers. "What about *Star Trek*?"

"Oh God." Any grain of attraction I had for him vanishes into the exhaust outside. "Look, I'll let you look it up online when we get back to the garage. I'm not a nerd. I don't know anything about *Star Trek* or *Star Wars*. I haven't seen any of them."

"No way." His head whips around to face me, his mouth open in horror. "We'll have to fix that."

"I'm not watching nerd shows." I shake my head slowly, back and forth, emphasizing my point. "I had to suffer through my brother's obsession with *Star Trek: The Next Generation*. I'm not interested."

"What do you like then?" he asks, shifting the topic away from his nerd obsessions. "Horror? No…wait, don't tell me. You like cheesy romantic comedies?"

"I like a lot of things. But I just watch whatever's on Netflix or Hulu. Amazon has some decent shows, but I don't really watch a lot of television. The shop keeps me busy."

"I have no idea what you just said."

With a sigh, I explain the slow evolution of how we consume media and the concept of streaming services. He nods like he understands, but I've seen that look before. Glassy eyes and stiff posture. He's completely lost.

"I'll show you online."

"What the hell does *online* mean?"

"On the internet."

"The what?"

I cover my face with my hand. This is complicated. "I'll *show* you once we get to the garage."

He nods and makes a right, turning onto my street. The garage's neon sign lights the side of the building. I pull out my phone and open the garage with my app.

"Neat trick," he says, bringing the car to a stop outside the shop, watching the slowly rising door. "When do I get one of those…uh, pocket computer-phone-things?"

"It's a smart phone." I tuck it away. "We'll get you one tomorrow."

With a nod, he pulls the car into the garage perfectly. Not a dent or scratch. The ride passed quickly and without incident. Dad wasn't lying—Cyril is a fantastic driver. I can see why he kept him on for so long. My father is notoriously picky when it comes to his employees…well, when it comes to everything really. It's part of his charm.

Cyril turns off the car and hands me the keys. "She purrs like a kitten and handles better than any car I've ever driven." His green eyes meet mine; a flash of dimple compliments his smile. "And I've driven a lot of cars."

"I'm sure you have."

"Seriously though," he says as he opens the door, "you've done a great job with her. Did you do the restoration yourself?"

"Yeah, took me a few years between other projects, but I'm proud of her."

He runs his hand over the hood. "She got a name?"

"No, why?"

"All cars treated with this much love and attention should have a name."

"I don't know." My mind blanks, and I shake my head.

"Think about it. A name will come to you." He runs his hand across the front end, tracing the lines of the hood with his fingertips.

A thousand dirty thoughts run through my head, but I swallow them all.

"Come on, I'll show you where Dad put your stuff in the attic." When I'm sure the garage door is secured, I flip off the lights in the shop and go through a door at the back. It opens to a staircase leading to the apartment above the garage.

Cyril follows me up the stairs. "They look exactly the same."

"You lived here?"

"Yeah. It was two apartments back then, but rent was decent."

I unlock the door, chewing the inside of my cheek. When I

took over the building, I combined the two apartments and moved in. It was easier than finding a place and commuting. Plus, I liked being close to my baby.

Inside, I toss my keys to the counter and head for the back of the apartment. There's a door leading to the attic where Dad stored all of Cyril's things, plus anything left behind when the last owner turned over the keys.

"It's all in here." I fiddle with the combination lock until it clicks open. "Have at it."

"Thanks." He leans against the wall and glances down the hallway. "So roommates, huh?"

Shit, I totally forgot about that. He quickly reads the expression on my face.

"If you're not comfortable with me staying here, I'll find somewhere else to crash."

"No. You're fine." I tie my hair up in a ponytail with an elastic band on my wrist. "I'll just clean the spare bedroom for you."

"You're sure?" His gaze holds mine, and his sincerity makes me pause.

"Yeah." I tap the attic door. "Grab what you need, and I'll get started on the spare room over here."

He acknowledges the room I point to. "Thanks again, Jessica. I know this isn't what you had planned."

"Story of my life." I shrug. "It's okay. We'll make it work."

Without waiting for a response, I head down the hall and flick on the light in the spare room. Just need to put some things away and then completely rearrange my life, but that's fine.

This isn't his fault. He didn't ask for this. I scold myself as I put loose clothes in a tote.

No one ever asks for it. But why am I always the one stuck cleaning up the mess?

CHAPTER ELEVEN
CYRIL

A chill wraps around me when I step into the attic. I flick the light switch inside the door to illuminate the space.

It's not huge, but I pause at the contents.

Boxes and tubs, stacked from floor to ceiling. Labeled with care and stowed away. My entire life reduced to the contents of this room.

My heart clenches, and I can't breathe.

Arthur could have thrown all of this away. But he didn't. He and Kate carefully packed every item and tucked it aside, just in case I came back. Their care and concern leave me overcome with emotion.

For Arthur to go so far as to give me the building…well, there aren't words to adequately capture the chaos inside me right now—hope, love, fear, desperation, and hovering over all of it, guilt.

Jessica is the reason all of this still exists. She brought my dream to fruition, even though she has no idea she did it. The woman has talent when it comes to business, I can tell that already. But her skill with cars? Incredible. I've never been more impressed by another motorhead in my life. What she's done with that Swinger takes time, patience, and dedication, on top of skill. Shit, it turns me on.

I push aside my blossoming attraction. There will be plenty of time to deal with it later. Right now, I need to sort through some stuff and get back to living. I start restacking boxes by type, searching for my clothes first.

Living with Jessica as roommates will create its own set of challenges. I've never been intimidated by a challenge before, but this one could be dangerous. I'm already attracted to her. And a soft spot in my heart is carved out just for her, because she's Arthur and Kate's daughter. I don't want to hurt her.

But I have a feeling it's going to be her doing the hurting.

She doesn't like me. I get it. It's a lot to take in over the course of a single day. I'm not sure I wouldn't be the same way if the shoe were on the other foot.

Reality is, I don't have a clue what I'm walking into in this new century, and I'm going to need all the help I can get. Jessica is the perfect person to show me, but doing so under direct order of her father probably wasn't the wisest course of action.

I don't know what game Arthur is playing, but if shit goes bad, this could blow up in all of our faces. Unease skates over me, but I shake it off. She deserves to know the truth about his plan. But there's no way in hell I can dump it on her today.

No. I need to get her to like me—or at the least, tolerate me. I'm on very thin ice here, and I'm not interested in seeing Jessica unleash her full fury.

If it were me, I'd be fucking pissed. This has to be handled with care, just like the bodywork on a vintage car. One small thing could completely fuck it all up.

A whoop of joy fills me when I uncover two boxes labeled *Cyril's Clothes*. I carry them to the bedroom and set them in the hallway next to the door. I find a few other items that might prove useful and add them to the stack.

At some point, I need to go through all of the boxes and decide what to do with everything. Right now, it's like I've found a time capsule. Maybe historians will want to be present for the unboxing of my personal possessions. Probably not. I didn't have much in '85, except a stash of *Star Wars* collector items. Wonder if they're worth anything now?

"Find everything?" Jessica asks from the other end of the hall.

"Yeah, I think so."

"Good. I'll let you get settled. Are you hungry?"

"I could eat."

"Pizza work?"

"Always." My stomach grumbles at the thought. "Thanks."

With a wave, she vanishes into the kitchen. I move the boxes into the bedroom.

The gray walls are bare, but there's a bed against the far wall, near the window, with a nightstand and a lamp. A tall dresser sits by the closet. On the other side of the room, there's a desk with a chair.

"What the hell is this?" I set the box on the bed and read the name on a black box sitting next to what looks like a small television screen on the desk. "Dell?" I make a note to ask Jessica about it later.

I unbox my clothes, wondering if I should wash everything before I put it away, considering how long it's been in storage. I check each item before deciding whether to wash it or put it away. By the time I make it through the three boxes, it's about even between a hamper behind the door and the dresser.

The last box holds an alarm clock, a few framed pictures, a Polaroid camera, and some books. Once I've emptied the boxes, I toss them in a pile to take out later.

"Pizza will be here in a few if you want to wash up." Jessica stands in my doorway.

I nod. "Where's the washer?"

"At the end of the hall, next to the bathroom. I'll show you."

I follow her with the overflowing basket. She gives me basic instructions, and I blink at the digital panel on the washing machine.

"Computers have taken over everything, huh?" I joke, tossing my clothes into the machine.

"You're in the digital age now." She grins. "Better get used to it."

"Let's just hope Skynet's not a thing," I mutter under my breath.

"Not yet, but there's still time."

"So you get a *Terminator* reference but want nothing to do with science fiction?" Damn it, this woman is a bundle of surprises.

Jessica rolls her eyes. "That's not what I said."

The urge to flirt is strong, but I bite back the instinct. Teasing flirtation can easily transform into button-pushing, and the last thing I want right now is to piss her off. It's weird though, knowing she's my boss's daughter and our ages are…yeah, it's a bit weird.

But is it?

Before I can dwell on it, Jessica leans close to press a button on the machine, and it whirrs to life. Her arm grazes mine. Warmth fizzles through me.

"Thanks." I move the basket out of the way to busy my hands.

"I'll give you a tour before the food gets here." She leaves the room before I can protest.

I know this place like the back of my hand. It might be renovated, but they didn't change the basic layout. I bite my tongue and follow her, admiring the soft curls lying against her sweatshirt, wishing I could see the curve of her backside again.

Her quick tour gets us only as far as the door by the time the doorbell rings.

"Shit. I'll be right back." She grabs some money off the counter and darts out the door, down the stairs to the side entrance.

When she disappears, I run my hand over my face. What the hell is wrong with me? I need to get my priorities straight. With thirty-seven years to catch up on, I shouldn't be thinking about Jessica and all of her delightful secrets and quirks I'd love to uncover.

The living room and kitchen sit directly over the shop floor. I lived here long enough to recognize the view through the wide windows overlooking the street below. The updated layout is spacious and welcoming.

I chuckle at a small cluster of plants making a jungle in the far corner of the room. What little direct sunlight there is will fill the space in the morning and afternoon. I used to have a chair in that corner. Never used it much, but I liked the way it perfectly caught the morning light.

Styles have certainly changed. Gone are the floral patterns, harvest golds and pea greens, replaced by neutral tones with pops of vibrant reds and blues. I pause at the gigantic monstrosity on the wall opposite me.

"That's not a television? It can't be." I step closer, admiring the sleek design and how much of the wall it takes up. It's massive. Like having my own personal movie theater! It looks like something straight out of *Star Trek*. Can you talk to people through it? See them? I search the sides for a switch or button, but if it's there, it's hidden.

"Alexa, turn on the television."

I'm surprised when Jessica reappears, but when the screen lights up, I stumble back, nearly tripping over the couch. My jaw drops. "How the hell did you do that?" I manage to right myself and clear my throat.

Jessica sets the pizza on the counter, her lips twisted in a half smile.

"Did you just talk to the television?" I stare at the screen, now filled with animated characters…no—animated children, cursing at each other. "What *is* this?"

"Alexa is a device linked to my network and the internet. Ask her anything, and she'll answer. Just use her name."

I glare at her. "And you told me Skynet wasn't real."

"The speaker is here." Jessica laughs and points to a box on the side table. "Or you can use the remote to turn on the TV, doesn't matter. That"—she points to the TV—"is *South Park*."

"*South Park?*" The words sound foreign in my mouth.

"Oh man, this is gonna be a long night. I need food." She opens the pizza box and fishes out a slice.

The smell hits me, and my mouth waters. "Giovanni's?"

She nods. "Been open for fifty years. Amazing."

I rush over and pull out a slice, letting the cheese slide and stretch. My eyes tear up. At least I have this. The first bite is exactly how I remember it. Perfection.

"Want a beer?"

"Yes, please," I say around a mouthful of pizza.

While she grabs two bottles from the fridge, I load my plate with two slices.

"Let's sit on the couch. I'll give you a crash course on entertainment evolution."

A shiver rolls through me, and I can't tell if it's fear or excitement. Either way, I'm committed. Maybe I can get her to put on one of the new *Star Wars* movies. I have a lot of catching up to do.

I take the beer from her and pop the top. She settles beside me on the couch, leaving a foot of space between us, even though there's more than enough room.

"Alexa, turn on Netflix." She turns to me with a glint in her eyes. "Hold on to your butt."

The screen loads, and then the clouds part while a chorus of angels break into song. It's fucking beautiful. I think I've died and gone to heaven.

CHAPTER TWELVE

JESSICA

Cyril looks like he's solved the ultimate question to life, the universe, and everything. His eyes are as round as vintage headlights.

I manage to stifle a laugh behind my beer bottle.

"So…" He sets aside the plate and stares at the screen. "This is Netflix?"

"Yeah. It's one of the first streaming services, although there are others."

"There are others?" He squints at me like he doesn't believe a word I'm saying.

"Paramount Plus, HBO, Amazon, Hulu…shit, the list goes on."

"You can just watch whatever you want? Whenever you want?"

I consider his question for a moment and shake my head. "Not really. It's complicated, but basically they need permission from the rights holder to showcase whatever they offer. Oh, and it changes all the time. Not a fan of that." I pout, remembering how they took *Friends* off Netflix a couple of years ago. Still kinda bitter about that.

"So I can watch *Star Wars* whenever I want?" His face practically glows.

"Well, you could for a while." I launch into a brief explanation of the evolution of entertainment since 1985. His expression is priceless.

"They don't make VHS tapes anymore?"

I shake my head.

"But they make…DVDs?"

"More Blu-ray, but that's a whole different thing. It's just easier to have a subscription to the streaming service and be done with it. Or you could buy a digital copy." Who knew forty years would have such big leaps in technological advancements for entertainment alone.

Cyril stuffs the last of his pizza in his mouth and chews thoughtfully while I skim through the selections. When I pass something familiar, he points, nearly bouncing with excitement. It's almost endearing.

"Can we watch a *Star Wars* movie now?" He wipes his hands on a paper towel before settling back against the cushions.

"I'll have to log in to Disney." I exit out of Netflix and choose the right app. I'm not interested, but honestly, it's worth seeing Cyril light up.

I can't imagine what it must be like for him, to wake up in the future, transported away from everything he knows. Everything he's worked for. I can sympathize with that. It's terrifying to think all your hard work could be wiped away without warning, to know you have to start all over again.

The screen loads, and I select the *Star Wars* icon. The selections fill the screen.

"Holy shit! What's the *Mandalorian? Rogue One? Boba Fett?!*"

"You really are a nerd." I hand him the remote. "Here, you can skim through everything. See what they're all about, although it might be easier to go online and do some research before you dive in."

"You keep saying *online*. What does that mean?"

With a deep sigh, I explain the birth and evolution of the internet as we know it, in the simplest way I can. No back history, no complicated threads, just my personal experience with the introduction of a personal computer in our home and the slow transition from analog to digital.

He soaks up every word like a goddamn sponge.

"So you're telling me, they use computers in cars now?"

"Yeah, it's a blessing and a curse. But I grew up with computers, so they make sense to me. We use them in the shop with the fleet."

"Fleet?" His eyes glow with interest. "How many cars?"

"A dozen. Keep them at a warehouse by the docks. Cheaper storage."

"How many drivers?"

"It changes, but we have a good team of fifteen drivers who rotate shifts and jobs."

"Damn." He whistles low. "That's not bad at all."

"We do most of the maintenance for the fleet at the warehouse. This shop is for custom jobs for high profile clientele."

"Spreading yourself too thin?"

I shake my head. "No, but the last two years have been a struggle. We're finally getting back on track."

"Is that why Arthur wants you to find a partner?"

My gaze fixes on him, even as a grumble of agitation builds in my chest. "That's why he *told* me I needed a partner. Then you dropped into my lap."

Putting Cyril and my lap in the same sentence should not have turned me on, but here we are. I shift uncomfortably and redirect the conversation.

"We can talk work tomorrow. I'll walk you through everything." My attention shifts to the television. "Tonight, let's just watch something and relax."

"Sounds like a plan." He swigs from his bottle, searching the screen again.

"What do you want to watch first?"

"Everything." He chuckles. "But honestly, I have all the time in the world to catch up. So pick something you think I'll enjoy."

A laugh escapes me. "I just met you this morning."

"True, but I trust your judgment."

His lopsided smile makes my stomach flip and my heart beat faster. Damn him and his charm. I take the remote from him, and my fingers brush his. Warm sparks crackle like fireworks, and I jerk my hand away.

"Static," I mutter under my breath. To my surprise, he says nothing.

Then it hits me. I know what movie he should watch first.

With the unexpected thrill of introducing someone to something new, I scan through my accounts until I find it.

"What's this?" A grin forms when he sees the gigantic red lettering on the screen. "*Jurassic Park*? Is this a dinosaur movie?"

"Only the best dinosaur movie ever made." I hit play and grab the blanket beside me. "It's my brother's favorite. He made me watch it over and over when we were kids. Had to sleep in his room for months after the first time."

"That scary?" Cyril asks.

"To a five-year-old? Yeah, it's fucking terrifying." The introduction begins, setting the scene.

His soft laugh sinks into me with the comfort of a warm towel straight out of the dryer. Which reminds me…I shoot off the couch, blanket flying.

"Where are you going?" he asks with obvious concern.

"I need to switch your laundry to the dryer."

He moves to stand, but I shove him back down to the couch. His chest is firm beneath my hand. I will not look closely at that observation right now. "Stay here. I got this."

"But it's *my* laundry." He pouts. "And you'll miss the movie."

"I've seen it a million times," I assure him. "I'll be right back."

The screaming of pissed-off velociraptors echoes down the hall behind me, and I shiver at the memories it conjures in my mind. No wonder I couldn't sleep alone for months. That sound is fucking haunting. The echoing cry of Muldoon's order chases the noise. I can picture the scene, frame for frame, as I pull the wet clothes from the washer and toss them in the dryer.

I hit start and dash down the hall, just in time to see the dig site come on the screen, followed by Alan Grant. Every time I watch it, I find something new. A detail I missed. A line of dialogue that takes on new meaning. It's one thing I love about rewatching old favorites.

"That's a hell of a way to start a movie," Cyril murmurs when I sit beside him. He offers me the blanket he'd stolen when I discarded it.

I take it and drape it over both of us, knowing full well I have a trunk full of perfectly warm blankets next to the couch. This one is big enough to accommodate two people without being squished together. Besides, his warmth will help hold the temperature beneath the blanket.

He shoots me a quick look when I join him under the blanket but says nothing and refocuses on the story unfolding on the screen. Our elbows brush, and when I shift, it brings us thigh-to-thigh.

The movie fades into the background as my brain spins a hundred miles per hour. I struggle to get it under control, to get my thoughts back on the road, but they're determined to pull a *Thelma and Louise*.

I mentally shake myself. This is crazy. I just met this man. His past and the complication of our present make this whole situation very delicate. I spent all afternoon fighting with my parents, and my better judgment, about why I should not let this man into my business, into my life. I know almost nothing about him.

I hazard a glance at his profile. He's fully invested in the movie, but he notices the movement of my head.

"Something wrong?" he asks, his voice low.

He's not flirting, but I'll be damned if his tone isn't causing a riot of butterflies in my stomach.

"No." I swat them away with a shake. "You like it so far?"

He nods and turns back to the movie.

There's nothing but us and the action on the screen. After a few tense moments, I'm sucked into the story. Just like I always am. This movie never fails to amaze me. I've memorized every frame, every line, but I'm always entranced by it.

As we watch, the story twists and turns. I know the jumps are coming, but I flinch every time anyway. I'm not sure when, but at some point, Cyril's arm is around the back of the sofa, in an almost protective posture. But he removes it after a few moments.

Am I disappointed by that? Or relieved? Everything twists inside me, and I'm even more confused when the movie ends.

The credits roll, and I seize the opportunity to fling the blanket back and stand, stretching my legs.

"You did good." Cyril also stands and arches his back.

Pride fills me, and I soak up his praise. "You liked it?"

"Loved it." He shrugs. "It's not *Star Wars*, but it's definitely a great movie."

I roll my eyes. "What is it about *Star Wars* that gets you all hot and bothered?"

"Have you seen Princess Leia in a bikini?" He laughs when I shove his arm. "I'm joking. Joking."

"Just for that, I should look up all the spoilers for the series and ruin the experience for you."

"Spoilers?" His eyes widen as he realizes the implication of my threat. "Don't you dare."

"Then don't be sexist."

"What? Han Solo is hot too. Should have given him his own shirtless scene, honestly."

I blink at him, twice, as his words sink into my brain. "Did you just say Han Solo is hot?"

"Yeah. Why?"

"Not many men would admit it." I straighten and smile. "I'm surprised, that's all."

"Guess I'm not like most modern men then." Cyril leans closer. His scent wraps around me, teasing me with a silent invitation. "And I'm full of surprises."

A strangled moan chokes me, but I manage to clear my throat and step away, snatching the blanket for something to do with my hands as I fold it.

"Well, I'll let you watch whatever you want. I'm going to take a shower and go to bed."

To his credit, he doesn't comment. When I walk past him, he gently touches my arm.

"What's that black box on the desk in my room?"

I think for a moment until my confusion fades. "A desktop computer. I can show you how to use it if you want."

"Please."

The simple word leaves me breathless.

After turning off the television and cleaning up the mess from dinner, I lead the way to his bedroom and power up the desktop. Once I give him a quick tutorial for how it works and how to access the internet, I let him take control of the mouse.

"If you have any questions, let me know."

"Thanks." He sits at the desk.

I pause in the doorway. "I'll set out a towel for you to take a shower."

"Sounds great." He turns to study me. "Thank you, Jessica."

His heartfelt gratitude sinks into my soul and chips away at the reservations I felt earlier at Mom and Dad's.

"You're welcome." I tap my fingers on the doorway. "I'm the last room on the left if you need me."

A sinful grin curves his lips, revealing those adorable dimples. "Got it."

Kicking myself, I retreat to the bathroom and take a long, hot shower. This man has turned my life inside out in only twelve hours. I can't imagine what tomorrow will bring.

CHAPTER THIRTEEN
CYRIL

My head hurts. No one warned me the internet is as addictive as cocaine.

I manage to drag myself out of bed, groaning at a quick glance at the clock on my nightstand. It's eleven a.m. I guess Jessica took pity on me. Either that, or she decided I wasn't worth the effort to wake. With a wary glance at the computer, I drag myself to the bathroom.

Last night, a half hour after Jessica introduced me to the glory of the internet, she returned to tell me the bathroom was free. I'm glad I seized the opportunity, because the moment I stepped under the hot water, everything crashed down on me.

The reality of my life. The situation I'm in. There is only one option. Embrace it.

Kate never found her way back to her time, so I'm willing to bet there's no way I can find my way back to 1985. It might not be what I want, but maybe it's exactly what I need.

When I returned to my room, I sat at the computer. After five hours on the internet, I've realized two things. One, this small piece of technology is a black hole; two, I need sleep to function as a human.

It's late morning, and the apartment is silent, but the hum of music and machinery pulses through the floor under my feet. She must be in the shop.

Grabbing an old pair of work pants and a dark T-shirt, I quickly dress. Thank God they didn't throw out my stuff. Arthur's forethought is saving me the hassle of having to hunt down clothes. With no credit cards, no driver's license, and no cash, I am at the mercy of my friend and his daughter. I tug on a pullover sweatshirt and snag a pair of work shoes from the bottom of a box I shoved aside last night.

When I step into the hallway, the haunting floral fragrance lingering in the air serves as a reminder of a woman I shouldn't be thinking about.

In the kitchen, I search for a coffee pot, but can't find anything even remotely resembling one. On the counter, there's a machine that says Keurig and a small tree holding plastic cups. Dark Roast, Light Roast, Espresso…coffee. I struggle with the machine for a moment, but once I turn it on, I'm able to figure out the process pretty easily—the advantage of understanding basic mechanics. I place a clean mug from the cabinet in position and push a flashing blue button.

The warm, intoxicating scent of fresh brewed coffee fills the air. Ah, technology.

From the deluge of information I tried to absorb last night, I've come to realize the future is both as bleak and as fantastic as I imagined it would be. But I could be biased due to the unnatural amounts of science fiction I've consumed over the years.

And still, the future is *nothing* like we predicted.

Coffee in hand, I head for the stairs. Today, I'm putting both feet forward. No use dwelling on the past. I can do this. No sweat.

My mental pep talk does little to silence a screaming panic in the dark parts of my brain. But somehow, I manage to push it aside by the time I reach the door to the shop.

Warmth hits me when I open the door, followed by the blasting sound of rock music and the familiar scent of grease and gasoline.

I make sure the door closes behind me, keeping a firm grip on the mug. Weaving around the toolbox and past the Swinger, I follow the sounds of metal clinking against metal and swear words drowning in guitar solos. My smile widens.

When I round the front end of the car—a modern monstrosity sort with a Ford logo—I pause. Jessica's legs peek out from under the beast as she lays on a creeper.

"Need a hand?" I ask before sipping my coffee.

The creeper's wheels squeal in protest as she slides into view. Her brows rise in shock. "You're alive?"

"You didn't warn me the internet would suck my soul out and keep me awake all night."

A grin splits her plush lips. "We all had to learn the hard way."

"Thanks." I grumble the word, but I'm sure she hears the sarcasm.

Slowly, she climbs to her feet and wipes the back of her hand across her forehead, leaving a streak of grease. Her dark blue tank top gives me an eyeful of bountiful cleavage, and I drop my gaze to the coveralls tied in a knot around her waist. Guess she got too hot.

If I stare at her much longer, I might spontaneously combust.

"Whatcha working on?" I tug at the collar of my sweatshirt and step to the side when she picks up the creeper and sets it against the wall.

"Oil change. Nothing special."

"What is this?"

"2013 Ford Explorer."

"It's a beast." I admire its bulk.

"Suburbans were all the rage in the late nineties and early 2000s. Still popular, although not as fuel efficient as other options."

"I take it there *are* other options?"

"You name the company, they make one."

"Interesting." I make a mental note to look up more information about the evolution of vehicles over the last three decades. It can wait though. Right now, I want to spend more time with her. "So what can I do?"

Jessica wipes her hands on a rag and tosses it on the toolbox. "Dad wants me to get your feet wet, so let's cut the foreplay. I'll show you the office."

Her choice of words isn't lost on me. I follow, admiring the sway of her ponytail against her shoulders. Does she realize I'm not immune to the charms of a woman who isn't afraid to get her hands dirty and call me on my bullshit? Every moment, it's getting harder to find a reason not to stick around and see where this leads.

Maybe Arthur was onto something? Or maybe I'll get my face bashed in with a hammer? It's a toss-up.

After our truce last night, when she introduced me to the delights of *Jurassic Park*, streaming services, and the cursed internet, there must be some foundation…at least for her to *not* hate my guts. We were laughing, having fun. Relaxed. Like friends, right?

It's been one day. Let's not expect miracles.

She opens the door to a brightly lit office with several desks, a wall of filing cabinets, and framed pictures of different vehicles from over the years. Walking past two desks, she leads me to a third and gestures for me to sit.

I obey.

Jessica reaches over and turns on the computer screen, wiggling the mouse as she withdraws. Her floral scent drifts past me, almost hidden beneath the pungent aroma of oil. The screen flares to life.

"You're gonna distract me with the internet again?" I chuckle, drawing her attention.

Her gaze flickers from my eyes to my mouth before she clears her throat. "Actually, I was going to show you the programs the company uses for scheduling, billing, filing, and maintenance records."

"You can do all of that on a computer?" I'm stunned when she nods. "How convenient."

"It is, actually."

"Then what are those are for?" I point to filing cabinets along the wall.

"Old records we've archived from before the shop went digital." She sits on the edge of the desk and uses the mouse to open an application on the desktop. At least I learned *something* during her lesson last night.

My mind drifts into dangerous territory again, and I force myself to focus on the screen instead of her. "How many employees?"

"In the office, four including me. Six on maintenance at two locations, and fifteen drivers."

"How many vehicles in the fleet again?" I lean forward as numbers come into view on the screen.

"Twelve, but I'd like to expand both the fleet and the number of drivers by the end of next year."

"How many are you thinking?"

"Two dozen vehicles and ten more drivers."

I whistle low. "You're determined, aren't you?"

"Well, the last two years were hell with the pandemic and the recession. People cut back."

"You're a luxury they could do without." I nod, understanding her position. Quietly, I file away details of her statements to look up online. Asking a million questions won't keep us focused on the task at hand. *Pandemic* warrants a closer investigation.

"Dad thinks I should expand, try to find new clientele."

"What do you think?"

Her bright eyes lock with mine. "I think we need to rebrand. As a chauffeur service, we put ourselves in a higher class, and while I think there's still a market for it, we're not against only the cabs now but also Uber and Lyft."

"What?"

Jessica sighs and briefly explains the two companies. Interesting. I anticipated the cabs would throw a fit at the encroachment on their turf, but healthy competition improves service, right? This information gives me incentive to find a way to expand the company in a way that benefits and brings positive engagement.

"Show me what you're thinking?" I grab the nearest chair and pull it beside me. "Sit down. Run me through it."

"Really?" She blinks at me, surprised. It takes her a minute, but she shakes off the stunned look and grabs a notebook from a drawer before sliding into the chair. "Get me a pen over there."

I select a blue ballpoint from the cup of pens sitting near the computer screen and hand it to her.

Her fingers close over mine. Heat radiates through my body at the simple touch. But as fast as it sparked, it vanishes when she pulls away.

For the next two hours, she walks me through her thoughts for Cyril's Car Service. I agree with her—rebranding the garage might be in our best interest. Showcase our flexibility and unique service. Maybe add a vintage touch, since it seems what is old is new again.

When the phone rings at two o'clock, I grab it out of habit. "Cyril's, how may I help you?"

Jessica arches a brow but sits patiently silent beside me.

"Cyril? It's Arthur."

"Arthur, what can I do for you?" I glance at Jessica, who tenses.

"I'm gonna need you and Jessica to do me a favor."

"Whatever you need," I respond with a smile. Just like old times.

Jessica grabs the phone and presses a button on the receiver. Her father's voice fills the space.

"What's up, Dad?" she asks, her tone terse.

"Oh, hello, sweetheart." He clears his throat. "I need you both to go upstate. Rob has some things he needs us to pick up for Marcy's party next week."

"You want us to drive to Uncle Rob's? When?"

"Tomorrow. Should be able to make it up and back in a day if you leave early."

Jessica grumbles under her breath, and I jump in. "We can handle that, Arthur. No problem."

"Good. I'll let Rob know you'll be heading his way in the morning."

"Is that everything, Dad?" Jessica clenches her jaw. If she keeps it up, she'll break a tooth.

"That's all. How's everything at the shop?"

"It's good. We're fast friends," I say before Jessica can respond.

She glares at me and shakes her head, but there's a sparkle in her eyes and a lilt at the corner of her lips, belying a smile and giving me hope what I say is true.

"Glad to hear it. Keep up the good work you two."

"Tell Mom I said hi. Love you, Dad." She nudges her father to say goodbye. I've heard that tone a million times.

"Love you too. Bye."

With our goodbye, she ends the call with the press of a button.

"We should finish here and get some sleep. It'll be a long drive tomorrow."

"I drive…drove for a living. That part doesn't scare me."

"Then what does scare you?"

"Leaving the city."

"Seriously?" She laughs, and the sound ignites heat inside me, tingling through my limbs.

"I've never left."

"Ever?"

"Ever." I stand and shove my hands in my pockets. "The only forest I've ever seen is the one in Central Park, and I refuse to walk through it at night."

Jessica stares at me like I've just sprouted a horn in the middle of my head. "Maybe this is a good thing. Get you out of your element."

"I was transported thirty-seven years into the future. I'm firmly removed from my *element*."

"Noted." She presses her lips together. "Come on. You can help me finish this oil change, then we can grab some dinner."

"Good. I'm starving. All I had for breakfast was coffee."

"Serves you right for sleeping in."

"Won't happen again." I round the desk and head for the door. She follows me, wearing an expression I can't quite place.

"Something wrong?" I ask, opening the door and stepping aside for her to exit the office.

"Nope." She brushes past me, and I'm surrounded by the scent of *her* again.

Tomorrow's road trip is going to be torment in more ways than one. At least I have a pretty copilot to distract me.

I just hope she doesn't kill me and bury my ass in the woods somewhere along the way.

CHAPTER FOURTEEN
JESSICA

Nothing ever works out the easy way. When Dad offered to let me take his truck, I should have known something would go wrong.

It wouldn't start. Of course it wouldn't. Why would it when he only drives it twice a year?

Cyril and I spent the better part of the morning troubleshooting the problem. Then we finally found it. A mouse must have chewed through part of the wiring harness. An easy fix, but I wouldn't have even thought to check for it had Cyril not mentioned it.

I'm used to plugging in a computer diagnostic tool and letting it do the legwork. But that's the problem with Dad's old pickup. No computer in this early-generation Dodge. I don't know why he insists on keeping it, but why does any old man do anything? Because he can.

Once we fixed the broken wires, she fired right up.

Then the clutch gave out.

Making an executive decision, I leave Dad's truck in the garage and opt for the Ford Explorer. By the time we get on the road, it's after one in the afternoon. We'll never make it to Lake George and back tonight. It's a four-hour drive one way, and knowing Uncle Rob, he'll want us to stay and visit. Shit.

Cyril offers to drive, but since he's never been out of the city, I take the wheel. He grumbles and pouts until I plug in my phone and set the map directions to Bolton. His eyes widen as we weave through the city with an automated voice leading the way.

It takes until we reach the other side of the George Washington Bridge for him to stop gawking at the phone every time it issues a new direction. Around the time we hit Interstate

87, he seems more comfortable, both with the ride and being outside the city.

"Is it how you imagined it?" I ask as we cross the state line from Jersey back into New York.

His attention remains fixed on passing scenery. It's hard to get a good look from the interstate, but the expanse of trees stretching across the horizon are definitely a change from the narrow view between skyscrapers and buildings in the city.

"Nope." He turns with a smile. "It's worse. How can you find your way in this chaos?"

"A compass." I chuckle at the horrified look on his face.

"Just don't break down out here, Peggy," he purrs to the Ford, rubbing the dashboard with his long fingers.

My gaze follows the way he strokes the plastic with an encouraging caress. I will not be distracted by this man. My grip tightens on the wheel, and I stare straight ahead. "Did you just name my car?"

"Technically, it's a company car." He sits back and relaxes. "And I did. She looks like a Peggy."

"Really?" I scoff.

"What's wrong with Peggy?"

"Nothing, I guess." My mind wanders to the soft tone he used while speaking to the car. It was almost…loving. I shake my head. "What made you pick it?"

"It was my mom's name." He turns away. "She died when I was ten."

Guilt slams into me. "I'm sorry."

"Don't be." He turns back with a subdued smile. "It was a long time ago."

"We have a few hours on the road." I shift to something more neutral. "I'm sure you have a million questions."

"I do." He cracks open a Coke he grabbed from the refrigerator at the shop and takes a sip. "But I don't want to bore you. I can look them up online later."

"Well, you don't have to ask me *all* of them. Maybe just pick the burning ones."

"What did you mean by *pandemic* yesterday?"

A heavy sigh rips from my chest. It's not a topic I like to visit, too many conflicting emotions and disappointments. But he deserves to know. I try to keep it as unbiased as possible as I explain, but the wounds are still fresh.

He listens and interjects with questions. For the first time in a long time, I feel like someone is actually listening to me.

The conversation drifts to other world events and societal milestones. When I mention 9/11, his eyes widen.

"That explains the skyline," he says under his breath.

"What do you mean?"

"When I was at the top of the Empire State Building to retrieve your mom's purse in 1985 and I got sucked into the…time slip or portal or whatever, and woke up in the present." His voice wavers. "The skyline was the first thing I noticed. Without the Twin Towers in the distance, I knew I wasn't where I should be."

"Oh." What do I even say in response to that?

"How old were you?" he asks.

"Eleven." I ignore the flashes of memories from that day.

He winces. "I'm sure that was horrible for everyone. Especially for a kid."

"It was. A lot changed." I launch into a brief history of our post-9/11 world. The war on terror, the restructuring of travel. The conversation slowly spirals into a dark and depressing void.

"Life wasn't perfect in the eighties," he says, as though trying to reassure me. "Every era has its problems and life-altering moments. That's how the world works."

"What, are you an amateur historian?" The break in heavy topics gives me a chance to breathe.

"No, but I always kept three books in the car while on duty. Most of them were historical nonfiction or sci-fi."

"That's quite a shift in reading material."

"I like to change things up. It's always good to have balance, don't you think?"

"I guess."

We pass a large green sign for the Albany exit. Only an hour left.

"So how well do you know Uncle Rob and Aunt Marcy?" I ask, moving on to lighter topics.

"We're not close, but I spent a lot of time with them before I ended up here."

His laugh makes me shiver with awareness.

"Marcy was a wild thing back in the day."

"Really?" Aunt Marcy has always been my favorite. She would take me for the summers, let me run wild on the lake. I got into all kinds of trouble, but she always bailed me out. "Tell me about her."

Cyril recounts the spring of 1985, when Marcy and Rob finally stopped clawing each other long enough to see the mutual attraction simmering between them.

"It was clear to anyone with two eyes and half a brain they wanted each other." He laughs at the memory, and part of me wishes I could have seen it. "She got caught up in a huge scandal with an up-and-coming movie star. It was in all the papers and tabloids."

"You're kidding?" I gape at him. "She never told me."

"I'm sure she has her reasons for staying quiet, but it's out there. It's probably on the internet if you want to read about it."

Cherished childhood memories of summers with Aunt Marcy and Uncle Rob fill my head. Do I really want to tarnish them?

"Or you can always ask her." He studies my face, and I warm under his gaze. "It'll be nice to see them again."

Relief fills me as he nudges the conversation once more. We started this partnership under less-than-ideal circumstances, and I had my reservations. How was I supposed to relate to someone from a different decade? The thought of holding a conversation with him left me in a panic. I'd rather smash my thumb with a hammer than be forced into idle chitchat with a dinosaur.

But he's not a dinosaur.

He's smart and funny. Most of all, he's perceptive. I've never felt so relaxed with anyone. Whenever the topic gets too heavy, he steers the conversation to something manageable. His intuition makes me think he's hypersensitive to those around him. Not an empath, but in-tune with life.

Is it really possible that, within only two days, I'm actually *comfortable* with Cyril? It seems crazy. But even more crazy is this simmering attraction between us. The soft tension nudging us closer with every exchange.

I want to hate it, but I don't.

Mom was right. Cyril is a great guy. But what does that mean?

I stuff aside the nagging questions and focus on the remaining thirty miles. Instead of diving back into conversation, Cyril turns on the radio and searches for a station he likes.

"You don't have to do that." I hand him my phone. "Look for the Spotify app. It's green."

I keep my attention on the road while he messes with the phone. "Found it." He taps the screen. "What is it?"

I push the button on the console monitor, and my phone connects to the Bluetooth. "You can pick one of the playlists or search for whatever music you want by title, genre, artist. Try it."

"You're serious?" His excitement fills the car. After a few seconds, Bon Jovi's "Livin' on a Prayer" filters through the speakers.

"Had to go with the eighties, huh?"

"I have a lot of music to catch up on." He waves me off. "Just drive."

I laugh. "You can't commandeer my phone indefinitely."

"Watch me." He cackles.

"Tomorrow, we'll pick up a phone for you, okay?"

His eyes light up like my nephew's when he got a PlayStation from my parents last Christmas. His innocent delight shifts into something more acute. Hunger? No, desire.

The sign for the town pops into view, and I sigh with relief. "We've made it. And just before dark too."

I make my way through town and find a quaint motel at the edge of the lake.

"What are we doing here?" He looks up at the *Vacancy* sign.

"Staying the night. I don't like to drive in the dark." I turn off the engine. "I'll text Uncle Rob to tell him we'll be over in the morning to pick up the stuff for the party."

"Sounds good to me."

"You hungry?" I reach for my phone, and he places it in my palm.

"Starving." His green eyes glint in the fading light.

Don't read too much into it, Jess. I fidget with my phone for a moment until my brain clicks into gear. Within moments, I send off a text to Uncle Rob and we head inside.

Lucky us, there's one room left.

With one queen-size bed.

Lovely.

CHAPTER FIFTEEN
CYRIL

I'm about to burst.

Between the information that's slowly been dumping into my brain and the delicious home-cooked meal from the diner down the street, I'm full to capacity. I can't possibly do anything but sleep at this point.

Jessica doesn't say much during dinner or on the short walk back to the motel. I kept my mouth closed when the clerk told us there was only one room left, with only one bed.

We're both adults. We'll figure it out. I thought about offering to sleep in the Ford, but with temperatures hovering around freezing, that would be stupid.

The town is quaint and homey. The shops have Christmas decorations in the windows, and lights strung across the main street cast a charming glow over the pedestrians. I glimpse an oversized Christmas tree in the town center with bright decorations and jewel-colored lights. It's not Rockefeller Center, but it's lovely and fits perfectly with the surrounding décor.

It's nice to be away from the city, but even if it weren't after dark, I'm not sure I'd be up for exploring. Maybe in the summer, but in winter, only a handful of days before Christmas, it doesn't sound like fun. I guess I can blame it on the lingering effects of time travel.

By the time we reach the room, I'm dragging. All I want is a shower and sleep.

"Are you sure this is okay?" I gesture to the queen-size bed dominating the room.

"It's fine." She shrugs. "I would call Uncle Rob and ask to stay there, but I don't think he wants Aunt Marcy to know we're here. He says it's a surprise."

"Won't she be home tomorrow when we pick the stuff up?"

"No, her quilting group meets at nine tomorrow morning. She'll be gone when we stop by."

Silence slowly fills the space between us.

"Mind if I take a shower?" I ask, moving toward the bathroom.

"Not at all." She pulls her phone from her pocket and flops down on the bed. "I'll take one after you're done."

I bite my tongue as an image of her joining me in the shower pops, fully formed, into my brain and expands like a hot-air balloon. Without replying, I turn and lock myself in the bathroom.

The narrow shower isn't built for two, which is a disappointment. I curse myself for allowing my brain to chase these details and cling to them for whatever twisted reason. Spending time with her has certainly increased my initial attraction, and I want nothing more than to sate my curiosity. What does she enjoy outside of cars? Does she read? The little things that are uncovered over time and with friendship—I want them now so I can better understand the woman in the other room.

Without lingering under the hot water longer than necessary, I wash and rinse. She's waiting to use the shower, and I don't want to be rude.

Once I step from the shower and dry off, I feel more comfortable. More relaxed. Wrapping the towel around my waist, I look at my reflection in the mirror. Damp hair hangs across my face, and there's nothing to block the expanse of my chest and arms from view. Shit. I forgot to grab my clothes before I came into the bathroom.

I double-check the towel secured around my waist. That's as good as it's going to get.

Opening the door, I peer around it to find her in the same spot, distracted by her phone. When I push it fully open, she looks up.

"I was worried you—" Her eyes shift from sky blue to midnight.

"Worried I what?" I ask, ignoring the hunger in her

expression as her gaze rakes over me.

"Drowned." She finishes before dragging her attention back to her phone.

I chuckle. There's something here. Chemistry. I'd bet money on it. What will happen if I lean harder on that mutual attraction? I'm not the kind of guy to press my luck, but I *am* trying to win her over. Maybe there's hope. All I can do is try.

She stands as I reach for my bag and rifle through it. When she brushes past me, heat grazes my bare skin. It takes all my effort to remain still and not turn, not reach for her.

I wait, even though the tension is killing me.

"Mind if I borrow your phone? I want to search something on the internet." I hold my hand out.

"Sure." She places it in my palm. "If I get any texts, just ignore them." Pink spreads across her cheeks and down her throat. She's blushing.

I barely have a chance to enjoy it before she retreats into the bathroom, forgetting to take her bag of clothes with her. I chuckle and cross to the small duffle bag she left on the dresser. I grab it and knock on the bathroom door.

"What?" she asks through the plywood.

"Your bag."

"Shit."

The door cracks open and her arm sneaks out. I slide the loop over her hand, keeping my gaze firmly fixed on the door between us.

"Thanks."

The barrier goes back in place as the door closes. I lean against it and take several deep breaths. Had she still been dressed? Was she in just a bra and panties? Was she naked, wrapped in a towel like me? Fuck. The question drives me insane.

I'm a gentleman. I stopped myself from looking. My wild imagination made the whole interaction worse.

Shoving away from the door, I try to redirect my thoughts.

Get dressed. Yeah. Clothes.

Setting her phone on the bed beside my bag, I pull out a pair of gray sweatpants I'd found in one of the boxes. They need to be replaced, but I can worry about it when I get back to the city. I forgo underwear and pull on the sweatpants.

I'm already hard thanks to the thoughts spinning in my head. My cock protests when I tuck it out of sight. Even underwear wouldn't hide the insistent bulge it insists on making. Fuck. She's going to take one look at me and know exactly what's going on in my mind. There's no denim to hide it. No oversized coats or long shirts. It's there, and I can't do shit about it.

I move the bag to the floor and sit back against the headboard. I cradle her phone in one hand and open the internet application. After a few minutes, I hear her turn on the shower, and suddenly my mind is filled with thoughts of her wet and naked in the other room. Fuck.

Redirecting my thoughts again, I type in *boomer* and hit search. A few minutes into reading an article, the phone dings and a message appears on the screen.

Ah, this must be what she meant by *text*. I ignore it and keep reading.

Three more texts come up, one after the other in quick succession. I try to ignore them, but when I try to swipe them out of the way, I accidentally open the notification. Shit.

Hey.

I miss you.

He misses you too.

A picture of an erection fills the screen.

"What the fuck?" I stare at the messages and the dimly lit image.

There's no denying it. That's a dick.

"Who would send something like this?"

The name at the top of the screen is Asshole Ex.

Ah. Well. That makes sense. But still, whatever happened to romance? Has it been reduced to impersonal messages and dick pictures? I shake my head in disappointment. Romance must be well and truly dead.

Another text comes through. This time, it's a photo of his dick with his hand wrapped around it.

Disgusted, I toss the phone aside at the same moment the

bathroom door swings open. She sees her phone flying through the air, landing on the comforter at the foot of the bed.

"Not a fan of the internet?" she asks with a laugh.

"It wasn't the internet." I cross my arms, wishing I had put on a shirt.

She grabs the phone and reads the screen. "Goddamn it."

I snort-laugh. Guess she isn't a fan of it either.

"I'm sorry about that. I should block him." She shrugs a shoulder, which pulls her tank top tight against her body, revealing a patch of skin just above the waistband of her pants.

"Is that how men flirt now? They send suggestive guilt trips and pictures of their junk?" Anger filters up. It's irrational and overwhelming, but I can't ignore it simmering through me. "He shouldn't send shit like that if you don't want it."

"He's harmless." She laughs and waves her hand. "Most guys at least wait for an invitation to send pictures, but there are a handful who like to project their confidence with dick pics."

Her words don't carry confidence. I study her closely, noting the way she chews her lower lip and nervously looks everywhere but at me.

"Want me to take care of him?" The offer leaves my lips before I can think it through. Hell, I'm not even sure what I'm implying, but she smile regardless.

"No, I took care of it."

"He's your ex?"

"Yeah." She sets the phone on the bed. "We still hang out sometimes, but it's nothing serious."

"You're telling me romance is dead?"

I rise slowly to my feet, and her gaze skims down the length of me, widening as it drops lower.

"It's not dead." She licks her lips and meets my gaze. The midnight storm in her eyes is back. Pupils blown wide, swallowing the color completely.

"You're telling me these guys sending photos of their dicks know how to flirt?" I step closer.

"I guess." She sways but doesn't otherwise move as I approach.

"They know exactly how to seduce you with words, their actions playing a perfect harmony to bring you to your knees." My voice dips, softening, deepening as I step into her space.

We're a half inch from touching, but I refrain. If she wants it, she'll take the next step. I hold my breath, craving it more than anything I've ever wanted in my life.

"Some of them." Her response is hoarse, laced with uncertainty.

"Do they know what *you* want?" I exhale, letting my breath skim her shoulder in a delicate caress. "Do they know what you *need?*"

Jessica turns, her lips parted, her eyes brimming with desire. "What are you trying to say?"

"Those idiots know nothing of romance."

"And you do?" Challenge echoes in those three little words.

"Yes."

"Liar." Her tongue darts out to wet her lips.

I'm burning, and only she can quench this desire.

"Prove it."

The moment her words register, I swear and close the gap between us.

Her lips meet mine, and there's nothing but her, me, and this fucking kiss.

CHAPTER SIXTEEN
JESSICA

What the hell am I doing? Kissing Cyril might just be the stupidest thing I've done since I told my ex I'd go on one date with him three months after we broke up.

There's no resistance from Cyril. He slides his arms around me, like they're meant to be there. I've never been a slim girl, and no one has ever classified me as petite, and in his arms, I feel like I'm a puzzle piece sliding into place at the end of a long, stressful struggle.

As if sensing the wandering thoughts in my mind, he tilts his head to the side. His tongue slides against the seam of my lips, begging for more.

My mouth obliges before my brain registers the danger ahead.

Why the hell does he taste so good? Cinnamon and sugar with a hint of cloves. I barely remember what dessert he had at the diner, but I don't remember it being nearly as alluring on the plate as it is on his lips.

Fuck it. Reason completely vanishes in the cold December night. I thread my fingers through his hair, pulling him closer as he ravishes my mouth. He kisses me like he's savoring the moment, savoring me.

Gone is the petty challenge I issued with my snarky comeback. Cyril has replaced it with pure need. It's almost as if he knew it was there, simmering below the surface, waiting to erupt with the slightest nudge. The idle curiosity of the last few days transformed somewhere along the way.

I'm Alice, lost in Wonderland, tumbling down the rabbit hole, and I have no idea what the hell is happening to me.

Cyril breaks the kiss. Our breath mingles in a rush of lost thoughts and absent protests.

His eyes, ones I thought were simply green, transform into a kaleidoscope of storm gray, moss green, and sky blue. Flecks of amber swim in the background. His pupils widen as he studies me. A Cheshire grin forms on his lips and his dimples reappear.

We stare at each other for a long moment, and my sanity begins to unravel in the silence.

"That was…" I lick my lips, searching for words, but they never come.

"Fucking fantastic." He completes my thought.

He's right. It was amazing. More than amazing.

I nod and tease my fingers through his damp hair. "Cyril…I…" Again my brain fails me, and I curse.

"It's fine." He hooks his finger under my chin and strokes my jaw. "Whatever you need, Jessica. If you don't want this, I understand."

"That's not it." Frustration and arousal spin inside me, creating a vortex of need simple sex can't touch. But nothing about sex with Cyril will be simple. It will be complicated as fuck. I don't know if I'm ready for the emotional and logistical fallout should we go down in flames.

"What do you need?" Cyril's smile keeps me grounded. "Tonight, you can have whatever you want, no strings attached."

"You don't really believe that, do you?" I laugh and his smile falters.

"Believe what?"

"That you can compartmentalize whatever this is. No strings attached doesn't work. Trust me, I've tried."

"Are you talking about dick pic guy?" He holds me firmly, his hands on my hips, his fingertips stroking the skin of my lower back beneath the fabric of my top.

"Yes," I grumble. His casual mention of my ex only pisses me off. Whatever happened with him has no place in this conversation. In this relationship. Leave it to Justin to overshadow my life, even when he's no longer an active part of it. Fucker.

"I'm not him." Cyril pulls me a fraction of an inch closer, rocking his hips against mine. I'm hyperaware of his shirtless state and the bulge pressing hard against my thigh through his sweatpants.

"I know. But it doesn't work that way."

"It works however you want it to work. I promise." Cyril leans closer and presses soft kisses to my cheek, trailing them gently along my jaw. When his lips brush mine, I capture them in another desperate kiss.

Passion spills free. I have no reason or desire to restrain it. It's been months since I last had sex, and my vibrator doesn't live up to the real deal.

And Cyril is more real than I've seen…ever.

He spins me around, pressing my back to his front. The hard line of his cock presses against my ass, and I arch back, earning a groan from him. He wraps one hand around the base of my throat.

I close my eyes and whimper, resting all my weight against him.

"Ah, you like that?"

I nod.

"Use words. I want you to *tell* me what you like…and what you don't."

"Okay." My voice trembles as he glides his thumb along my throat.

"Good girl."

My knees buckle, and he catches me around the waist. His soft chuckle skims over my neck.

What exactly has he been looking up on the internet? The thought crosses my mind, but before I can ask, he rests both hands on my hips and hooks his thumbs in the top of the elastic band around my waist.

He pushes the fabric down. My face heats when he drops to his knees, eyes level with my ass, and urges me to step out of the pajama pants.

I look over my shoulder to find his gaze searching for mine. "Cyril."

"You want me to stop?" he asks.

"No."

"What do you need?"

The repeated question lingers in my mind, and I still don't have an answer. All I know is the heat building inside me needs release. And if he doesn't give it to me, I'll take it myself.

"You're thinking too much." He slowly rises to his feet. "Tell me what's rolling around in your lovely head."

"I need to come." In all the years I've dated, I've never felt comfortable voicing my sexual needs. I've always known what they were to an extent, but I've never had a partner I trusted to seriously consider them.

"How do you want to come?" He leans close, his words burning my mind, his breath teasing my flesh. "On my hand? My tongue? My cock?"

I take a deep breath. "Your tongue."

"Good answer." His eyes light up. "I've been dying to get my mouth on your pretty little cunt."

The harsh word throws me off for a moment, but I shake it off as he gently guides me to the bed. I settle in the middle of the mattress. He climbs between my thighs, lifting, spreading, feasting with his eyes.

A growl rises from deep in his throat as he settles into place. His hot breath teases my center before he drags his tongue over me. A moan rips from my throat, echoing off the walls. His eyes meet mine as he repeats the action. Shivers roll through me, and my legs fall wider on the bed. He smiles, and I lose all sense when his tongue descends once more.

My hands fist in his hair, twisting and pulling with every wicked pass of his tongue over my sensitive folds. He's a master, teasing my clit with gentle nips, suckling briefly before releasing pressure. I'm a writhing mess. He pins one hand on my stomach, keeping me still beneath him.

When he slides two fingers inside me, I buck off the mattress. "Fuck."

His laughter is drowned out by my panting curses. With every stroke of his fingers and lap of his tongue, my pleasure spirals higher. Just when I think I can't take any more, he adjusts his position, shifting his attention away from the oversensitive area.

He's teasing. Edging.

Fucking hell, I want to strangle him.

"May I…" The request comes in gasps from my lips. "Please."

"What?" he asks between licks. "I can't hear you."

"Let me come," I growl, desperation making me more agitated. "Please."

Pleasure spirals hotter and faster. I can't take much more of his torment. If I don't come soon, I might lose my mind.

Cyril takes my clit in his mouth, laving his tongue over the swollen bud. His fingers stroke deeper, harder, rubbing my inner walls, creating delicious friction. When he hums, the world shatters.

My climax overtakes me, dragging me under in waves of pleasure. He doesn't relent or release as I tremble beneath him. I rock my hips against his mouth, savoring the sensations slowly ebbing into the dull pulse of my retreating orgasm. My eyes close as my body shivers.

The bed shifts, and I rouse when he settles beside me, wrapping his arms around me. I snuggle into his warmth and note the hard length pressed to my thigh.

"Want some help with that?" I ask, reaching to palm him through the fabric.

He groans in my ear and thrusts his hips. "I won't say no."

I roll over, facing him and reach into the waistband of his sweats. His cock fills my hand, overflowing my grip. I stroke his length, noting the way he sucks in breath between his teeth, then groans when I squeeze the tip.

"Fuck, that feels good." He shifts to his back when I remove his pants and straddle his thighs. "Take off your top," he instructs me.

I strip the tank off, loving the way his eyes widen and those dimples appear when he sees my tits for the first time. I've always thought they were too big, but when he reaches up and takes them in his hands, I stand corrected. They fit perfectly.

His disappointed groan when I pull away is replaced by a

satisfied grunt as I take him in my mouth. He's bigger than I'm used to, but I suck and tease, raking my teeth gently over the ridges.

"Fuck, Jess. I can't remember the last time…" He moans when I run my tongue over his head like a sucker. "It's been forty years."

His laughter disappears into the background of my mind when reality sinks in.

Forty years. Cyril is from 1985. He worked for my father. Dad's forcing us to work together. Forcing this partnership.

And here I am, choking on his dick like a good fucking girl. Oh, hell no.

I jerk back and climb off him.

"Where are you going?" Cyril sits up, confused, completely naked, his cock at full attention. "What's wrong?"

"This. It's…" I snatch my tank top and my pajama pants off the floor.

"It's what?" He rises, climbing slowly off the bed. "Did I do something? Say something?"

"No." I tug the top over my head, hiding my tits from his view, and struggle to pull on my pants. "I shouldn't have kissed you."

"Wait, what?" He grabs his sweatpants and pulls them on, grunting when they restrain his hard cock. I almost feel bad for him. Almost. "What just happened?"

"You don't belong here." I round on him. "You belong in 1985."

"Thanks for the reminder." He scoffs, a scowl marring his handsome face. "But there's nothing I can do about it. I don't have a time machine. I can't snap my fingers and go back to the life I knew. I'm here. Now. Whether I like it or not."

"That's not my problem," I snap.

"It is now." He steps closer, and I take the same steps back.

Fury pounds through me. Resentment for my father. Cyril. Mom. Life.

This isn't how it's supposed to go. All my hard work, gone in a flash. And wouldn't it just be the icing on the cake to fuck me while he fucks me over?

Cyril pauses and flexes his hands. "Look. I don't know what happened or what I did, but I'm sorry. Okay."

"Are you sorry?"

"Of course. I never meant to hurt you."

"Really?" The dam slowly cracks, and I feel pressure pushing forward at an alarming rate. A rate I'll never be able to counter. Instead of biting it back, I embrace the flow as it bursts free from the depth of my soul.

"You walk in, and Dad welcomes you with open arms. He gives you a position in the company—in *my* company. A job. An apartment. Everything." I glare at him. "I worked my whole fucking life to make him proud of me. To get him to believe I could run the car service and the garage without his meddling. Without someone hovering over my shoulder, telling me what to do and how to do it."

Cyril straightens, his expression impassive. "Is that what you think I'm doing?"

"Aren't you?"

"No. I didn't ask for any of this, Jessica."

"You might not have asked for it, but you're in the middle of it."

"I'll walk away right now if it will make you feel better. But I think you should talk to your father first."

"Oh sure, make yourself a martyr. Poor Cyril." The hateful words spew from a dark place in my soul, and I cringe when he flinches.

"That's not what I meant." He sighs. "Or what I want."

"What do you want, Cyril? Do you want to steal everything from me? Including my shop?"

"I don't want to steal anything. I don't want the shop." His shoulders slump. "I just want you to be happy."

Fuck. I pull my hair in frustration. "Look, I'm sorry. It's been a long week. I'm obviously not in a great place, and pushing this into a physical relationship is probably the worst idea in the world."

"We can't deny the chemistry here."

"No." I agree with a nod. "But I can't act on it. I was wrong to kiss you. To put you in this situation and then pull away."

"Takes two." He shrugs. "I know what you mean, and I understand."

"Maybe we should just go to bed and start fresh tomorrow." My conscience takes a dive the moment the adrenaline wears off.

"Yeah. Okay." Cyril walks around me to the bathroom. "I'll give you some time alone."

"Thanks." I turn and watch him close the door behind him.

The moment the barrier seals between us, I collapse to the bed. Tears flow. What the hell just happened? What is wrong with me?

I like Cyril. I want him. Crave him. But he's a threat to everything I've worked so fucking hard for.

Can I trust him?

The shop is my baby. It's my dream. Where does he fit into this? Does he fit?

I grab a tissue and wipe my face before ripping back the blankets and climbing into bed. Once I'm nestled under the covers, staring at the wall, my mind races.

What happened between us? I wanted it. More than anything. Then why did I stop it? Why did these intrusive thoughts come barreling in at the worst possible time to ruin the moment?

I scream into the pillow before repositioning it under my head.

The faint sound of running water comes through the bathroom door. Is he showering again? Or is he taking care of the hard-on I gave him, so he won't have to sleep next to me with blue balls and a battered conscience?

I cringe. I'm the worst fucking person. I should apologize, talk it out with him. But shame has wrapped its claws around my neck. I can't do it.

Five minutes later, I hear the bathroom door open and pretend to be asleep. When the bed shifts, I hear his sigh as he lies down beside me.

My apology chokes me, and we fall asleep in strangled

silence.

CHAPTER SEVENTEEN
CYRIL

I should have slept in the car. The cold and discomfort would have been equally matched to sharing this room with Jessica. I wake up before dawn, after struggling to sleep for most of the night. Finally, I give up, get dressed, and take a walk by the lake.

Jessica never moves.

The air is crisp and cold. There's a bite to it, like it wants to snow but can't. It's two days before Christmas, and I can almost imagine this place coated with a dusting of white, turning it into a winter wonderland.

With a sigh, I keep walking, soaking up this little paradise. For a moment, I forget I'm not in Central Park. It's almost freeing.

It's surreal. All of it. Being here, in this place, at this time.

But that's not what's eating me alive. It's her. The way she makes me feel. The way she's burrowed beneath my skin. The way I don't want anything as much as I want her. Not just sex. *Her.* Her company, her laugh, her sass. She's determined and smart, but there's so much more she's hiding, keeping firmly locked away.

I was so close to unwrapping those layers, to revealing her depth. Then she pulls away and closes herself off, snapping at me with such venom, it left me stunned. What the hell did I do? What happened?

Halfway down the trail around the lake, I turn around and slowly make my way back to the motel. A breeze pushes at my back, making me pick up my pace. I need a hot cup of coffee and something to eat.

What I truly crave is the woman who's got me twisted in knots.

She's afraid. That's obvious. This isn't only about the garage or who runs it. No, this runs deeper. I'm not a psychologist, but I know what it's like to have someone threaten to take away the one thing you love. It fucking sucks. When it's gone, the world feels hollow and empty. Life fails to have meaning. But there's always hope. If I found it, she can too.

How do I convince her I'm not going to take anything from her? What I want from her isn't the garage. It isn't tangible. It can't be bought, sold, or monetized. How the fuck do I convince her I want *her* and nothing else? That's the real question.

Frustration churns in my gut. By the time I reach the motel, I still haven't found a solution to my problem. All I can do is give her space, let her breathe.

My hand rests on the knob, and I pause. Fuck. I still remember how she tastes, the softness of her skin. I'm hard just thinking about her soft moans and whimpered curses. I spent thirty minutes in the bathroom trying to will my cock to relent. Finally, I caved, took myself in hand, and jerked off with the water running, hoping she was asleep and wouldn't hear me grunt when I came to thoughts of her. Goddamn it.

When I open the door, the scent of coffee hits me. I look for her, but the bed is empty and the bathroom door is open. Everything is packed, including my stuff. Shit. There's a coffee cup sitting on the table next to my bag. I pick it up and see my name on the side. I groan with the first sip. Warm and rich, it instantly soothes the caffeine craving.

The door opens and Jessica appears in the doorway.

"There you are. I thought you got lost in the wilderness." Her teasing comment alleviates some of my hesitancy.

"Just took a walk. Didn't want to bother you." I lift the cup in my hand. "Thanks for the coffee. I needed it."

"I picked up pastries too. They're in the car." She motions to the door. "Uncle Rob just called. He dropped off Marcy at the Senior Center, so we're in the clear to pick up the stuff."

"Right." Once I grab my bag, I do a quick scan of the room to make sure we didn't forget anything.

"I already double-checked the room. Your bag is the last

thing to go." Jessica opens the door and holds it for me.

"Thanks," I say as I brush past her.

The sweet, tantalizing scent of her soap mixed with the heat of her skin leaves me aching. I'd give anything to pin her against the wall and taste her again. Make her cry out my name when she comes against my mouth.

Instead, I sip my coffee and make my way to the car.

The ride to Rob's place takes less than five minutes. We pull up to a quaint Victorian off the main street. Jessica parks in the short driveway behind the home.

I manage to stuff the remaining pastry in my mouth before getting out of the car.

Jessica leads the way to the house and knocks on the back door. A few moments pass before it swings open.

Holy shit. I expected it after seeing Kate and Arthur, but Rob's full head of gray hair and weathered squint behind bifocals stop me short. My heart breaks at seeing a man I admired so altered by time and life. I keep forgetting how many years have passed since I last saw him. Feels like yesterday to me, and yet, the man before me has lived a full life since then. I swallow a lump in my throat as Jessica greets him with a hug and a kiss on each cheek.

"Uncle Rob…" Jessica turns, but she stops when Rob steps down to the landing outside the door.

"Cyril." His eyes widen and fill with tears. "As I live and breathe." He claps me in a hug, squeezing me tight with a strength that belies his age.

"Rob." I bask in the warmth of his greeting. "It's so good to see you."

He pulls away and studies my face with an expression of awe. "When Arthur called and told me...well, I couldn't believe it." He grips my arm tighter. "I'm so glad you're here now. We were worried."

"Yeah, sorry about that." I run my hand through my hair.

"You're safe. That's all that matters." He steps back inside and motions for us to follow. "Come in. Would you like something to drink?"

"No, thanks." I follow Rob and Jessica into the hallway and close the door behind me.

The interior is not what you'd expect in a traditional Victorian home. The rooms have been altered to open the space. The kitchen and eat-in dining area are off to one side, the living room and office to the other, with a staircase and hallway bisecting the home neatly in half. The décor perfectly reflects its occupants. With Rob's background as a physician and Marcy's flair for fashion, the home represents them equally with a strange but fluid balance.

Rob steps into the living room and gestures to a sofa across from the oversized recliner he commandeers. "Sit. Relax. Take a moment to breathe before you get back on the road."

"We can't stay long, Uncle Rob."

He waves his hand. "You never visit me."

"You come to the city all the time," Jessica says before sticking out her tongue.

He mimics the action. "You've always been a brat."

"I learned it from you." Love sparkles in her eyes when she says the words. They truly have a unique bond.

Rob's knowing gaze drifts between the two of us, sitting beside each other. His lip twitches.

"So I take it Arthur filled you in on what happened?" I ask, diverting the conversation before it has a chance to take root.

"He did." Rob strokes his jaw. "I must say, I'm a bit surprised."

"Why?"

"For years, Kate has maintained her story. She traveled through time from 2020 to 1985." He scoffs. "It was a hard pill to swallow...the thought of time travel and all that."

"You believe her now?"

"I believed her then, only because there was no other explanation for the things she knew." He winks. "But now...now I'm positive it's true. Look at you! You haven't aged a day."

"Not sure if that's a good thing or not," I joke, unable to meet Jessica's curious stare. I feel it burning the side of my face as she studies me.

"The boys at the Black Penny aren't going to believe it's you next week at Marcy's birthday party." His bark of laughter echoes through the room, and I laugh with him.

"Do you have the stuff for the party?" Jessica asks.

"It's in the garage. You can grab it on the way out." He chuckles. "Marcy has no idea. We've been planning this for ages. Jackie reserved the whole bar for us."

"Does Claude still own it?"

"No. Retired years ago. His daughter, Jaqueline, runs it now." He leans back in the chair. "Yup. Claude and Gwen retired to a quiet place in the Poconos. Grant and Quinn bought a nice home in Brooklyn where they run a nonprofit for foster kids."

"That's great." Hearing these details pulls at my heartstrings. I've missed so damn much. "What about you and Marcy? Do you enjoy it up here?"

"We love it." He heaves a contented sigh. "We moved here in '86. I had a small practice for twenty years until Marcy told me to retire so we could travel. By that time, the kids were out of the house."

"You have kids?" I stare, gobsmacked.

"Two. Nicholas and James."

"Talk about brats," Jessica grumbles under her breath.

Rob laughs again. "You should've seen the five of them running around this place in the summer. It was pure chaos."

The conversation continues, and I slowly absorb the details of the family's lives. I missed so much. After an hour, Rob leads us to the garage and helps us load some boxes into the back of the Ford.

Jessica shuts the hatch. "We're ready to roll."

"Sounds good." I turn to Rob and offer my hand. "Thanks."

"You're family, Cyril." He wraps his arms around me and holds me tight. "If you need anything, give me a call."

"Yes, sir."

"Take care of my niece, would you?"

My gaze meets Jessica's. "Always."

There's a flash of pink in her cheeks before she spins around, heading for the driver's seat. "Love you, Uncle Rob," she calls as she opens the door.

"Love you!" Rob shouts back and nudges me with an elbow. "Be patient. She'll come around."

His whispered comment lingers in my brain as he retreats to the house. I climb into the Ford. "Want me to drive?"

"No, I got it." She puts the vehicle in gear without looking at me.

The ice wall between us has refrozen. Damn it. My mind spins as we drive out of town and back to the highway, heading south. I have four hours to break the wall down. But how?

Music plays through the speakers to dispel the silence between us. The phone periodically interrupts, giving us directions, but after two hours, I can't take the tension a moment longer.

I turn down the volume, and her grip tightens on the steering wheel.

"What's going on?" I ask.

"I don't know what you're talking about."

"Yes, you do." I exhale a half-exasperated sigh. "Last night—"

"What happened last night was a mistake. It won't happen again."

"Which part?" I pull at the fraying edges of the conversation, unraveling like a threadbare blanket.

"All of it."

"Ah. We're not going to discuss it like two mature adults?"

"What's to discuss?"

Her attention remains fixed on the road, and I'm relieved her hands are occupied because I'm pretty sure she'd throw something at me if it would shut me up. Judging from the tone of her voice and the rough edge to her words, she's not interested in discussing anything concerning *us*. I let the faint music fill the silence, creating a soothing reprieve from the tension.

"When I was a kid, I wanted to be a race car driver." The words spill free. Words I haven't voiced since I was young.

Somehow, it feels right. I keep going. "Dirt track. No rules. No worries. Just the purr of the car and adrenaline coursing through my veins."

Jessica doesn't say anything, but she's listening. It's a start.

"My dad left when I was five. Mom worked three jobs to keep our apartment. When she died, I went to live with my Gram, but her place wasn't much nicer. There were rats, and bullies lived upstairs." My gaze fixes on the highway in the distance, losing focus and drifting back to those horrible years when we had nothing.

"I stole my first car when I was fourteen." The confession hovers in the car like an overfilled balloon, threatening to burst. "By the time I was eighteen, I'd been arrested four times. Gram had given up on me. Called me a lost cause."

"I was twenty when your father caught me trying to steal a car."

Her attention shifts to me for the briefest moment before returning to the road. She says nothing, but I can almost feel the gears churning in her mind.

"He just happened to walk past at the right moment. Caught me red-handed." I pause to let the words sink in.

"What did he do?" she asks.

"He gave me a choice." I smile as the memory appears in my mind, like a movie on the big television in her apartment. "Work for him or go to jail."

"He offered you a job?" She shakes her head. "How could he possibly trust a thief?"

"I don't know. Maybe he saw something in me. Maybe he felt bad for me." I shrug. "Who knows? I never asked him why he did what he did."

"Why are you telling me this?" she asks.

"I want you to know who I am."

"Why?"

"Because I want you to trust me."

She scoffs. "Why should I do that?"

He takes a deep breath. "I'm not here to take anything from you—not the garage, not your parents, your apartment, your life."

Silence meets my statement, so I continue. "I want to make this work. This partnership." My heart thunders in my chest. I hope she'll take the olive branch I'm offering. "You're a hell of a mechanic and a damn savvy businesswoman. I'm here to help, but you have to *trust* me."

"And if I don't?"

"Then it makes this ten times harder than it needs to be."

With a nod, she turns up the radio, and the conversation is over.

I shift, leaning against the door, staring at the passing landscape. I don't know how to get through to her. How to make her understand I'm on her side. I want her, *need* her to trust me. Otherwise, this is going to be miserable for everyone.

Fuck.

By the time we reach the city, the sun is setting. She pulls into the garage and turns off the ignition.

"Need help?" I ask, climbing from the car.

"Nope." She slams the door.

I get it. She needs space. Time to process everything. I leave her in the garage and retreat to the apartment upstairs to finish sorting through my past, still piled in boxes.

When she's ready, she'll talk. I hope.

All I can do is pray I didn't fuck this up beyond repair.

CHAPTER EIGHTEEN
JESSICA

I can't avoid him forever. On Christmas Eve morning, I creep into the kitchen to make breakfast, careful not to wake Cyril. When we got home last night, I busied myself with work in the shop.

After the disastrous road trip to Uncle Rob's place—including the insanely hot encounter in the motel—I put distance between Cyril and me. I had to. There was too much going on in my head…and in my heart. I need time to think.

I'm stunned by his confession about his background. Revealing those vulnerable tidbits about his past left me wondering who he really is and how much my father truly knows about him. Why do I feel like there's something bigger at play here? It could just be my cynical nature.

I don't trust easily. I'm skeptical of everyone and their motives. I have to be. I'm a woman who owns her own business, living in the city. If I want to succeed, I can't be taken in by a handsome smile or flirty charm.

While the coffee brews, I make some oatmeal. It's not my typical breakfast, but it'll hold me over until we get to Mom and Dad's. Since before I was born, they've hosted a family holiday meal with all the trimmings. This year is no different.

Except for Cyril. They invited him to join the festivities as part of the family.

I'm dreading it. The first thing I'm going to have to field is my siblings' awkward questions and knowing winks. They're both happily married and have hounded me for years about my love life. Would it shut them up to think Cyril and I are dating? Probably not. They'll rip me apart the moment I walk into the house.

What's so wrong with Cyril? He's handsome, smart, and

hardworking. His sense of humor is ten times better than any other guy I've ever met. All in all, he's not a bad choice. He's nearly everything I've ever wanted in a man.

Except he wants my shop for his own. He says he doesn't, but I can't stop this nagging suspicion he'll drop me once he gets what he wants from my father.

Why does the thought of his rejection sting so much?

His kiss lingers in my mind, tormenting me. The stolen moments of pleasure follow me like a thief in the shadows and invade my brain without warning. Was his confession sincere? Does he really care that much?

We've known each other less than a week, but being in his company is easy and relaxing. Even having to introduce him to the twenty-first century wasn't nearly as big a trial as I'd imagined it would be. He's taken everything in stride and assimilated into modern culture in a surprisingly quick period.

"Good morning," Cyril says from the doorway. His hair is rumpled, and he's wearing an gray eighties-style sweatshirt with matching pants.

For a moment, I'm back in that motel room with the tension crackling between us. *Girl, he's a thirst trap.* I shake the thought from my head and finish the last of my oatmeal.

"Morning." I jump down from the stool and carry my bowl to the sink. "Want some coffee?"

"I got it." He crosses the kitchen, brushing my elbow as he passes.

"You figured out the Keurig?"

He drops a pod into the chamber and closes it with a soft click. "Yeah, it's a clever little contraption."

"Hungry?" I ask, unable to replace the hard-won distance between us.

"Not really. Coffee should do the trick."

I glance at the microwave clock. Nine twenty-five. "Mom wants us at the house by eleven thirty. Gotta help her make Christmas Eve dinner."

"Oh. I wasn't sure if you wanted me to go or..."

"Mom and Dad requested your presence. You can't back

out now." I put the excuse firmly on them. The last thing I want this morning is Cyril realizing I'm no longer angry with him. The truth is much more unnerving, something I'm not prepared to examine too closely.

A soft smile touches his lips as he lifts the coffee mug. "I don't want to impose."

"You're part of the family." I clear my throat and sip my warm drink. "According to them."

Fortunately, he says nothing. I watch as he crosses the kitchen and retreats down the hall. Damn him. I wanted to keep that wall between us, but without effort, he manages to chip away at it.

By eleven, we're ready to leave. I let him drive the Swinger. It's supposed to rain later, but there's no snow in the forecast, so we should be fine. We arrive a little before noon and have to fight for parking. Of course we're late. Hopefully, my siblings are keeping Mom and Dad distracted. I know the grandkids should be.

Cyril steps out of the car. He looks like a model selling a slice of the past in his eighties suit and coat, standing next to my '74 Swinger. I should take him to get an updated wardrobe.

Wait, why am I doing anything?

Because you want him.

My brain shorts. Goddamn it.

The moment I walk in the door, chaos descends around me. Christmas music drifts throughout the first floor. The thundering of feet overhead tells me the kids are playing in the spare bedroom. Overlapping voices drift through the hallway. The scent of spices lures me deeper into the house.

I pause to hang up my coat, and Cyril follows suit. I catch a grin on his lips as I turn. Ignoring the flutter in the pit of my stomach, I tighten my grip on the bag in my hand—gifts for my nieces and nephews. I never greet them empty-handed, even if it's only their favorite chocolate.

When I peer around the corner, I spy my brother and brother-in-law sitting on the couch. Dad sits in his chair opposite. The television is on, playing *It's a Wonderful Life*. A small

Christmas tree glitters in the corner by the front window.

"Hi, Dad."

"Jess. I didn't hear you come in." He shifts forward, scrambling from his chair to stand. He hugs me, smiling when he sees Cyril. "Glad you both could make it."

"Thank you, sir." Cyril shakes his hand firmly.

My brother, Matthew, stands, as does Steve. They hug me and shake hands with Cyril after Dad introduces him.

"I'm gonna go help Mom in the kitchen."

"Sandra and April are in there already," Matthew says with a smirk. "They're cursing your name."

"Of course they are." I hand him the bag for the kids. "Put this under the tree."

When I reach the kitchen, Mom's laughter is filling the air. "There you are," she says when she spies me in the doorway. "Good. You're just in time to finish these pies."

I greet everyone with hugs and kisses.

"Where's Cyril?" Mom asks.

"He's with the boys in the living room."

"Who's Cyril?" My sister spins, spatula in hand.

"No one, Sandy."

"Wait…he's the guy Mom was telling us about. The time traveler." She sets the utensil aside and wipes her hands on her apron. "I need to see this guy."

"Me too." April follows her out the door.

I hang my head and start rolling out pie crust. Their questions will come in a flurry, and nothing will stop their curiosity.

Mom sets some pie pans down beside me and pats my arm. "Are you okay?"

"I'm fine." Forcing a smile, I meet her concerned gaze.

She squints like she doesn't believe me but sighs and waves her hand. "Your father had the house in a state this morning. Jimmy and Nate…" She chatters on about her two oldest grandchildren and a search for Grandpa's box of treasures.

Grateful for the distraction, I listen and work. Dad keeps a special box of mementos hidden in the house, adding to it occasionally with treasures he finds during his travels. The kids love hunting for it every time they come over, hoping something new appears.

The moment April and Sandra return, it's a flurry of questions. I fend them off easily enough, and Mom steps in, telling them to give me some space. I'm thankful for the reprieve, but I know they'll come at me again at some point today.

We fall into a familiar rhythm of making food. Rotating dishes through the oven with the precision of a well-run maintenance shop. By four o'clock, we've picked through the appetizers and drunk a huge bowl of sparkling punch. We set the table for dinner, then sit as a family precisely at five.

Cyril sits beside me, and I can feel my family's eyes on us both as we eat. My nieces and nephews are suspiciously quiet and well-behaved. I wonder if my sister and brother slipped their children chocolate this afternoon, hoping the sugar high would wear them out. I'm pretty sure it was grandma's fruit punch and chocolate chip cookies that pushed them over the edge into sugar coma though.

The meal flows without incident. It's nice to sit comfortably with my family and enjoy their company. I'm fortunate to live close to them all, to see my nieces and nephews growing up, to spend time with Mom and Dad. I'm a lucky woman.

Then there's Cyril. Sitting beside him, I'm reminded just how relaxing his presence is, like a warm blanket on a cold rainy day. Even without speaking, he puts me at ease. I *should* hate it. It's like I'm waiting for the rug to be pulled out from under me, and yet, there's nothing there but calm contentment.

Maybe he was telling me the truth and he just wants me to be happy. No strings attached.

After dinner, we open gifts and help clean up. Cyril and I are the last to leave. It's raining when we step out onto the stoop, and raindrops, splashing into puddles, reflect the streetlights around us.

Mom and Dad wave from the front window, and I smile as I get in the car. I was worried about today, but it ended up perfect.

Well, almost perfect.

Soft Christmas music plays through the speakers, filling the car's interior. I hum along, some of the lyrics slipping free. Cyril drives, his attention fixed on the road, hyperfocused on the conditions. Droplets spatter the windshield. Streetlights glow in the rain, creating halos of red and green light.

When he pulls up in front of the garage, I reach for the opener. He rests his hand on mine, nudging it away. He turns off the car.

The rain pelting the roof of the car and the thundering of my heart fill the silent void. I lick my lips, wondering what's going on inside his head. The neon light above the garage casts a surreal glow over the car. I track rain rivulets across the windshield.

"You really love this place, don't you?" His question startles me.

"I do." I focus on the building, but every ounce of my being is fixated on this man beside me.

"You've done well. Made something special."

I choke up.

"I'm not going to take anything you're not willing to give me, Jess." He takes my hand and turns it palm up. My body tingles, and warmth pools in the pit of my stomach. He places the keys in my palm. "I'll leave as soon as I can find a place."

I blink at him. What the hell is he saying? "You're leaving?"

"You've made it clear you don't want me here. And I won't stay if I make you uncomfortable."

"You don't make me uncomfortable."

I put my hand on his and draw him back. His gaze rests on me. The glass fogs from our warm breath in the cold and rain around us.

"I like having you here."

He threads his hand through my hair and pulls me to him. "Are you sure?" His lips hover over mine.

I'm desperate for him. "Yes. Please."

Then I'm drowning in his kiss beneath the patter of Christmas rain, and the last of my reservations wash away.

Chapter Nineteen
Cyril

Every uncertainty disintegrates under these pliant lips that cursed my existence.

I need her. Crave her. We're steps, moments, away from being upstairs in a warm, welcoming bed, but it's fitting to be here, in her car.

Breaking the kiss, I reach down and pull the lever. The bench seat slides all the way back. She chuckles at the sudden jerk as it locks into place.

Heat reflects in the depths of her blue eyes, drawing me closer, telling me she wants this as much as I do.

With as much grace as I can muster, I slide across the bench. She pivots, allowing me to sit in the passenger seat, and straddles my thighs. I curse the thick fabric hiding her body.

"I'm pretty sure this is illegal." Her heat sinks into me as she peels my coat open.

I push her heavy coat from her shoulders. "Does it matter?"

"No." She finally pulls my coat free and tosses it to the back seat. "But we could go inside."

My body is on fire with every movement. Her hips against mine. Her mouth against my jaw. Her fingers against my stomach as she fumbles to unbuckle the belt.

My hands come to a rest on her hips. I've managed to get her coat off, but if I don't contain the desire vibrating through me, this will be over before it starts.

Once I get her in a bed, I'll explore every inch of her. Right now, I just need to be inside her.

"Something wrong?" she asks, nipping my earlobe with her teeth.

"Not a goddamn thing."

"Then why are you shaking?" She hums, and I close my

eyes. "You can touch me."

"It's been a while, Jess." I meet her gaze. "If I touch you, it won't be soft or gentle."

"Who says I want soft or gentle?" She reaches into my pants and strokes my cock.

"Fuck me," I mutter under my breath, and she laughs. "I won't last if you keep this up."

"We've got all night." She kisses me, and I'm lost.

The taste of sweet red wine lingers on her lips. I drink my fill, savoring the way she meets my hunger with her own, tangling her hands in my hair.

Hooking my thumbs into her waistband, I tug her soft leggings down, and she shimmies, maneuvering enough to get them to her ankles. She reaches back to pull them off with her boots, as though she's done this a million times.

My hand glides along her thigh until it brushes her damp panties. I press the fabric to her clit. The scent of her surrounds me. Her taste is still in the forefront of my mind from the night at the motel. I slide my fingers beneath the fabric and coat them in her arousal.

When I bring my finger to my lips, the action drags a moan from deep in her throat.

"You taste so good."

"Damn it, Cyril." Her eyes are dark midnight storms of need. "If you tease me—"

"I'm not going to tease you." I pull my cock out, rub the head across the heat burning between her thighs. "I'm going to fuck you."

"Then stop talking and do it."

She rocks her hips against me. I see stars as the pleasure sparks desperate desire.

"Condom?" I ask.

She shakes her head. "No. I want you like this."

"But—"

"Do you trust me?" She rests her hands on my shoulders. At my nod, she smiles. "Good. Now fuck me like you hate me."

I laugh. Her lips cover mine, swallowing the humor,

converting it to pure heat. She nudges the panties aside and lowers herself onto my cock.

The moment her body closes around me, I nearly lose all restraint.

My body trembles at the force it takes not to go deeper. Then she rolls her hips.

I fucking lose it.

Clawing at her back, I grip her tight against me as I drive deep. Over and over, thrust after thrust.

She arches her back, gripping the door for stability. Our heavy breaths steam the windows.

It's only us. This car. This moment.

I love it. Treasure it.

Her hand slips, slides across the foggy glass. I press her hand flat against the window, letting the cold seep through our overlapped fingers. The only outward sign of what's happening inside the car.

She rides me, hard and fast, chasing her pleasure. I release her hand and press my cold fingers against her clit, rubbing slow circles.

Her movements turn frantic. She grips my shirt in her fists.

I barely glimpse the rush of pleasure on her face as her orgasm hits. Her head tips back, eyes closed, lower lip between her teeth, moan vibrating from deep within her.

She's fucking gorgeous.

I give in to my own release. It rushes me in waves until I'm completely spent.

Jessica rests against my chest. "That was a first."

"What do you mean?" I stroke her back with soft rhythmic movements.

"Never had sex in a car before." She leans back and studies my face. "Have you?"

"A few times." The memories refuse to come, but I know I have. Guess it never mattered before. "But never in a '74 Dodge Dart Swinger."

She scoffs and tries to move away. I hold her tighter.

"This is by far the best sex I've had. Let's leave it at that," I murmur.

"I'll agree with that."

We sit in silence for a moment. The rain slows to a gentle patter on the roof of the car.

"Maybe we should go inside."

"Sounds like a good idea. I'm getting a cramp in my calf." She rubs her leg as she climbs off my lap.

After we manage to somewhat cover ourselves, I hit the garage opener button and climb into the driver's seat. She fishes the keys off the floorboard and hands them to me.

After we park the car into the garage and secure the doors, Jessica grabs me by the arm and pulls me to the stairs.

"Ready for round two?"

I chuckle. "We haven't even recovered from round one."

Halfway up the staircase, she glances over her shoulder. "You too old for this?"

"I never said that."

Inside the apartment, she tosses the keys on the counter and spins to face me. Mischief dances in her eyes.

"What?"

"If you'd stayed in 1985, how old would you be right now?" she asks, resting her hands on my hips and pulling me closer.

Mental math was never my strong suit. "Mid-seventies."

"That's a hell of an age gap."

"I doubt you'd want an old man."

"Guess we'll never know." She grabs my ass and squeezes.

I cup her jaw and kiss her. Soft. A tender exploration I neglected when we were in the car. She melts against me.

Methodically, we pull off each other's clothes, a slow reveal of skin as we make our way down the hall. Articles of clothing litter the path we take. Our lips brush, our teeth clash with every tumbling movement.

Somehow, we manage to make it to her bedroom without breaking anything.

Jessica flicks the switch, and a lamp beside the bed comes on. Soft light floods the room. The only thing I see is her, naked, climbing onto the queen-size bed. The teal comforter is plush beneath my hands as I follow her.

She lies down, wrapping her arms around me while I cover her body with mine.

Finally. Skin to skin. She's a perfect complement of curves against me. We're like two puzzle pieces, strewn across different decades. How we found each other still amazes me.

Her kiss lingers between panting gasps as I explore her with my fingertips. She rakes her nails across my back, over my arms, down my hips. When she takes my cock in hand, I'm ready for her.

"Jess," I murmur against her mouth.

"What?" She strokes me twice. My head spins.

"I lo—"

She kisses me, stealing the words from my tongue.

Maybe it's too soon. Not the right moment. But those words linger in my mind. They've never felt more true than they do right now. I love her. Call me crazy, but I can't deny it. Whatever this is, it will always be love to me. Nothing else makes sense.

I wedge myself between her thighs and press into her. It's like coming home. She wraps her arms around me and locks her heels around my legs.

There's no hurry, no desperate need. Just a slow unfurling of pleasure as we move together.

If what we did in the car was fucking, then this is making love.

My hands glide over her smooth skin as I take my time with easy, measured thrusts. She meets me with equal hunger, her hands unable to stay in one place. Our lips explore every inch of flesh we can reach.

I roll her onto her stomach and pull her hips up. When I drive deep, her gasp of pleasure shakes the walls. She pushes back, meeting each movement with resistance. I grab her hips, her breasts, her thighs.

When I sink my teeth into her shoulder, she tightens around my cock.

Doing it again, I find her clit and stroke it, teasing to make her sputter curses.

"Damn you." She pants and grips the comforter.

"Do you want to come?" I ask. She's close. I can feel it.

"Yes."

"Ask me nicely."

Jessica glares at me over her shoulder.

"One word. That's it." I roll my hips, hitting the spot I know she likes because her breath catches every time.

"Please."

My pace quickens, and it doesn't take much to tip her over the edge. When the orgasm rips through her, she screams my name.

I've never heard a sound so goddamn sweet.

I follow her down, my climax tearing through me before she can pull away. She doesn't though.

We settle on the blanket, and she curls against me.

"Thank you," she murmurs into my chest.

"For what?"

"Staying."

I tighten my hold and kiss her head. "Thank you."

"For what?"

"Letting me stay."

She chuckles. "Merry Christmas to us."

Chapter Twenty

Jessica

Waking up next to Cyril on Christmas morning is the best present I never expected.

He curls tight around me, holding me close, burying his face in my hair. His hand cups my breast, kneading it like a kitten making biscuits. I can't tell if he's still asleep or in a weird, half-awake state of consciousness. I rock my hips back against him, and he returns the motion.

The sunlight through the window tells me it's later than I think it is. Not that it matters. I don't have anywhere to be today.

Honestly, there's nowhere else I'd rather be than in bed with Cyril, hungover from multiple orgasms and zero sleep.

It was totally worth it.

"You awake?" I ask softly, afraid to break the spell hovering in the room.

"Mm-hmm." He nuzzles closer and huffs in irritation. "Your hair is a nuisance."

Brushing my curls out of the way, he settles his lips beside my ear and takes the lobe between his teeth. The gentle tug leaves me aching for more.

"How are you still horny?" I chuckle when he grinds his cock against my ass.

"What can I say? It's all you, baby." He kisses my cheek.

"Sure." I wiggle against his hold, but he only tightens his grip and turns me to face him.

Those mesmerizing eyes hold me captive. There's teasing, but also an honesty that leaves me breathless. I cup his cheek.

"I'm sure this wasn't how you expected to spend Christmas," I tease.

"No, but I'm not complaining."

"Is there anything special you want to do today?"

"Aside from lying around naked with you? Nope." A flash of teeth and those matching dimples warm my heart.

"We can't lie around naked all day."

"Why not?" He grips my hip, stroking his thumb over my skin in gentle circles.

"We have to eat. And I don't think it's wise to cook without clothes on. Unhygienic and dangerous to…certain parts of your anatomy." I wrap my hand around his cock.

He sucks in a breath. "You have a point." His groan vibrates through me as I stroke his length. "What do you want from me?"

"Is that a rhetorical question?" I bite back a grin when he moans.

"I guess. Maybe. I don't know. It's hard to think when you're playing with my dick like that."

"Want me to stop?"

"Fuck no." He sighs. "But I'm gonna need food if you want to keep tormenting me."

I release him. "Let's go make something to eat."

He dramatically flops back on the bed when I climb out of reach. "Fine. You win."

Cyril watches me as I pull on some Snoopy Christmas pajama bottoms and a warm long-sleeved shirt.

"You covered all the good stuff."

"Exactly. Less distraction for you." I laugh and head for the bathroom.

Once I've taken care of the most demanding necessities, I return to find the bed empty. He's not in the bathroom or his bedroom. I venture further down the hall, following sounds of movement in the kitchen—the clinking of pots and pans, the slamming of cabinet doors. What in the world?

I round the corner to find Cyril wearing gray sweatpants and a dark blue short-sleeved shirt. He's got a carton of eggs in one hand.

"How do you feel about French toast?"

"I love it."

"Good." He beams as he sets the eggs next to a glass bowl. "Where's the cinnamon?"

I slide past him, resting my hand on his shoulder, and reach for the cabinet behind him. His gaze follows me as I retrieve the spice and put it next to the eggs.

"Do you want help?" I ask, leaning against the counter.

"I won't say no to a sexy companion in the kitchen." He lifts the fork and points it at me. "But no fondling while I work."

I lift my hands and smile. "I can't promise anything."

"You're saying we can't work together without you wanting to touch this?" He runs his fingers down his chest.

"I guess not."

He chuckles and cracks the first egg. "I thought so."

"At least let me put on some music." I turn toward the living room. "Alexa, play my Christmas playlist."

Cyril shakes his head when music fills the room. "That machine is witchcraft. I love it." He leans close and whispers, "Do you think she listens to *everything?*"

"Probably." I bite my lip to keep from laughing. I wonder if she did hear everything we did last night. Weird thoughts form in my mind…what would an AI do with that information? I shove the thought aside and focus on Cyril as he whisks the eggs and milk together.

I grab bread from the pantry and open the bag.

"The pan is hot. Go ahead and make the first couple. I'm gonna run to the bathroom."

"Okay." I turn when he heads for the hall. "Hey, can you grab my phone from the bedroom while you're back there?"

"No problem."

Alone with Christmas music and the sound of sizzling French toast, I relax. This is nice…whatever *this* is. I chew on my lip. What is this? Better question is, what do I *want* it to be?

My short marriage ended in flames, and my relationships after that weren't fantastic either. I'm not interested in diving into something else. Relationships didn't work in the past, why would one magically work with Cyril?

Because he's not like them. He's different.

That's what they all say.

Relationships are complicated…messy. I've finally got my

life where I want it. Focused on me and my shop. Nothing else matters.

And yet, here we are.

I flip the toast as they reach the perfect golden-brown crisp. That's when my brain does a one-eighty.

What if Cyril is different? What if he's what I need to get this business to where it should be? What if he's exactly *the man* I need? Not just as a business partner, but as a romantic partner? I've never before had a connection this strong with anyone in any capacity. It's strange and wonderful…and absolutely terrifying.

I don't want to take a huge leap of faith only to land in a big pile of shitty disappointment. Damn it. I'm fucked either way. It's too late to turn back now.

After taking the crispy pieces of toast off the pan, I dip more bread in the egg mixture and start the process over again. Lost in my thoughts, I weigh my options.

Just ask Cyril. Talk to him.

It sounds so simple, and yet how the fuck do I bring this up without sounding like an absolute asshole?

Tell him how you feel.

And then watch him walk away.

The words linger in my mind longer than they should. When Cyril appears, bearing my phone in hand, I straighten and shake the uncertainty from my thoughts.

"Thanks." I take the phone and tuck it into my pocket.

"Your dad called. I answered it. He said he only had a minute but wanted to wish us a Merry Christmas."

"Oh. Yeah. He's taking Mom out for a special brunch today." I smile even though nerves twist in my stomach. "Did he say anything else?"

Like did he say anything about you answering my phone? Or ask if we finally hooked up? Just the thought of my father piecing it all together leaves me uncomfortable. I love my parents, but they don't need the details of my sex life.

"He said he'll call back later." Cyril takes the spatula from my hand and nudges me to the side. "These look great. Maybe I should let you finish cooking. I always burn them."

I take the spatula back and push him out of the way. "I'll finish this part. Why don't you get syrup and butter from the fridge?"

"Yes, ma'am."

His response leaves butterflies in the pit of my stomach. I watch him out of the corner of my eye as he works. I like this.

I like *him*. A lot.

Okay, more than a lot.

Fuck. Do I love him?

The question doesn't scare me like it would have a few months ago. What the hell is going on?

"Where are the plates?"

I point to the cabinet with the dishes.

"Cyril?" I ask, my voice hesitant.

"Yes?"

I bolster my courage and push on. "After last night, what's the plan?" I sigh. "What do we tell my parents?"

He pauses, his arms raised halfway to the shelf. "I haven't really thought about it."

"What do you want out of this? From us?"

He removes two plates and closes the cabinet before turning to face me. "I guess that depends."

"On?"

"On what you want." He steps closer, and his presence makes my body light up like a dashboard of error codes on the fritz.

"That's the problem. All my previous relationships, I thought I knew what I wanted, but I was wrong. I don't know if I can trust what my brain says I want."

"Then we take it slow. Double down on the partnership with the shop. Let it run its course, see where it leads in six months. Sound fair?"

"Yeah, it does. And this?" I rest my hand on his chest and meet his smoldering gaze. "Can we keep this part?"

"The roommates-who-fuck part?"

"Yes." I lick my lips. "Or am I asking too much?"

His sigh vibrates through me.

"I won't lie. I'm already half in love with you. Might break my heart in the end, but I'll agree to it, if that's what you want."

I can't tell if his tone is serious or teasing. His expression is guarded, but there's a mix of humor and honesty there.

"I don't want to make it awkward." I drop my hand. "We don't have to…"

"No, it's fine. We're beyond awkward at this point." He picks up the plates, one in each hand. "Can we eat now? I'm starving."

With a laugh, I put three pieces of toast on each plate and turn off the stove. We sit at my small table and enjoy lighter conversation as we eat. Even with the heaviness of unanswered questions between us, there's comfortable companionship.

After breakfast, he helps me clean up and we retreat to the living room. I retrieve a small package from under the tree and place it in his lap.

"I got you a present."

He stares at it in awe. "You didn't have to do that."

"I did. Open it."

When he unwraps the present, he laughs while he removes a familiar box with an Apple logo.

"You bought me a handheld computer-phone thingy."

"Close enough." I point to it when he pulls the phone out of the box. "It's already set up, and I've programmed our numbers into it. Everyone you know is in there."

His eyes glint with unshed tears. "Thank you."

When he presses the home button, he laughs at the image that pops on the screen. A rugged close up of old-school Han Solo. He holds the phone up and points to it. "Really?"

"It's your favorite series, and you told me how hot Han was." I sigh. "Harrison Ford is absolutely Daddy material."

Cyril chokes and bursts into laughter. "Oh God. No."

"What? Don't like me calling an older man who's not my father *Daddy*?" I jab him in the ribs.

"No."

"Should I call you *Daddy*?" I nudge him again.

"Absolutely not."

"Fine." I huff and reach for the remote. "But now you've asked for it."

"Asked for what?" He narrows his eyes.

"I'm going to introduce you to the Daddy of them all."

"Please no." But his curiosity gets the better of him. "Who are you talking about now?"

"Bruce Willis." My heart goes a little wobbly. "I've had a crush on him since I was twelve."

"The guy from *Moonlighting*?" Cyril scrunches his nose up. "And that's a highly inappropriate age difference. Twelve? Seriously?" He shivers. "Why were you drooling over older men at twelve?"

The pointed look I spear him with shuts him up immediately. "Considering the age gap between *us*, I wouldn't talk. I wasn't even *born* until 1990."

"Point taken." He gestures to the TV. "As long as you don't refer to him as *Daddy*, I think I can handle whatever you have to show me. What is it?"

"Only the best Christmas movie ever!" I turn on the TV and find *Die Hard* on one of the many streaming services I subscribe to.

"Wait? This is a Christmas movie?" He balks when he sees the movie poster on the screen. "This looks like an action flick. *Rambo* or something."

"Oh, it's something. That's for sure." I snuggle close to him, pulling the blanket over both our laps. "You're gonna love it."

I press play and bask in the comfort of a film I've seen a hundred times, mindful of the fact that Cyril has never seen it.

That doesn't stop me from grazing my hand over his cock.

Or slipping it free and taking it in my mouth.

His hand tightens in my hair as he watches the movie, his body responding to each stroke of my hand, of my tongue.

"Fuck." His breath hitches as McClane reaches the Christmas party.

Redoubling my efforts, I tip him over the edge and swallow every drop.

"Goddamn." He takes a minute to recover his breath. "That was amazing."

"The movie isn't over yet." I refocus on the pristine white tank top-wearing cop and grin. "We're just getting started."

Yippee ki yay, and Merry Christmas to us.

CHAPTER TWENTY-ONE
CYRIL

The past two days have made the loss of thirty-seven years worth every stolen moment.

Jessica and I have reached a truce. Gone is the hesitancy, the uncertainty between us, replaced by something fragile and priceless. Over the course of Christmas and the following day, our tenuous relationship is transformed.

We spent most of the time in bed between movies and meals. I've never been so content in my life. She slowly revealed bits of herself between orgasms and laughter.

If I weren't already head over heels for her, I certainly am now. It solidifies the decision I made Christmas morning when I woke in her arms. I nearly told her, but there's no reason to rush. We have time.

Pulled from our domestic bliss, we finally relent to the demands of reality on the morning of the twenty-seventh. Marcy's party. Arthur called at seven a.m. to remind us to be at the bar by noon to decorate.

He didn't know was I was already awake with my head buried between his daughter's thighs. I mean, he *did* throw us together so we could come to an agreement. He might not have meant romantically, but part of me believes he hoped this would happen. Forcing two people to spend time together is a surefire way to ignite sparks already flying between them.

Outside the Black Penny, Jessica parks the Ford and pops the hatch. My gaze drifts over the familiar brick building. It looks mostly the same. The only difference is the neon lights have been replaced by a brighter, bolder sign hanging over the door.

"Carry this in." She places a box in my arms.

Stunned, I follow her into the bar. The lights are up, brighter than usual. I chuckle when I look around. The inside hasn't changed.

Well, the jukebox has been replaced with a digital replica. The floors have been refinished, as well as the bar. But otherwise, time hasn't touched the Black Penny. I'm grateful. It's like a little piece of home.

"Jess!" a woman shouts from behind the bar.

"Jackie!" Jessica slides her bags onto the nearest table. "God, it's been forever."

"It has." The woman rounds the bar, her short hair brushing the top of her shoulders. "How have you been?"

I watch as the two women embrace and fall into conversation. Hanging back, I listen, only taking in bits of information. Rob and Arthur said Claude's daughter runs the Penny now. Is this her?

Judging from the balance of her curves and height, her dark hair, bright blue eyes, and a healthy sprinkle of beauty marks across her skin, I'd say she's a perfect blend of Claude and Gwen. She's a knockout, but I'm distracted by Jess's laughter. Something in my chest does a little flip when I catch her glancing at me.

I smile.

"Who's this?" Jackie asks, turning to me.

"Cyril?" A deep voice echoes from the back of the room.

We all turn to find a small group slowly spilling into the bar. As with every reunion so far, my heart breaks to see the passage of time etched in every gray hair and wrinkle on those familiar faces.

Claude and his brother Grant step closer. Gwen and Quinn stand to the side, whispering to each other.

"Surprise." It's the only word I manage to say past the emotion choking me. I worried they were gone and I would never see them again. While this isn't the reunion I imagined, I embrace it.

"We thought you were dead," Grant says, shoving his hand into mine and shaking it before pulling me in to clap me on the back.

He releases me, and Claude mimics the action. "When

Arthur told us, we couldn't believe it."

"Well, now you can see for yourself." I clear my throat when Gwen and Quinn shove their husbands aside and rush to embrace me.

I grin at their overlapping chatter. I missed them. All of them. I address their questions one at a time until I'm breathless.

"It's almost one." Jessica appears at my side and elbows me in the ribs. "Dad will be here soon. We need to finish setting up. Uncle Rob and Aunt Marcy will be here at two."

Everyone bursts into a flurry of activity. Claude and Grant help me hang streamers while Quinn and Gwen give Jackie a hand with the food. Jessica sets the tables, placing a favor on each plate. Uncle Rob had them made especially for her birthday.

As I work, I'm drawn to her. She lights up the room like sunshine on a summer day. I can't soak up enough of her energy.

Claude smiles when he catches me staring, but he doesn't say anything.

We've nearly finished when Arthur and Kate arrive. Jessica helps her mother retrieve a few more items from the car before offering to move it so it won't spoil the surprise.

I kiss Kate on the cheek, and Arthur nods a greeting. When his wife wanders off, he pulls me to a small nook beside the bar, out of earshot.

"Are you sure about this?"

"Absolutely." Confidence bolsters my tone.

"Okay." He hands me a sealed envelope. "It's all yours."

"Thanks, Arthur."

I look up when the door swings open and Jess steps inside. She's grinning. I suck in a breath.

"You're in love with my little girl." Arthur's quiet observation echoes between us. It's not a question. "I didn't think it would work, but I'm glad it did."

"You set us up?" I spin to face him.

"Of course I did." He claps his hand on my shoulder. "All those years I trusted you as my driver, my right-hand man. How could I not see the advantages of you officially joining my family?"

"Let's not jump the gun, Arthur." I scoff. "This is all new. It might not work out."

"It'll work out." He winks. "Trust me."

"I don't know. She gets a stubborn streak from her old man."

His laughter draws the attention of everyone in the room. I nearly hide my face, hoping they have no idea what we're discussing.

"It doesn't matter." Arthur waves his hand. "I know you'll treat her right, regardless of what happens down the road."

"Always, Arthur." I tuck the envelope into my sports jacket pocket.

"Grandpa!" A little girl shouts from the doorway and rushes Arthur for a bear hug.

Over the next thirty minutes, the bar fills with people. Kids. Grandkids. Friends, old and new. I'm surrounded by people and caught up in a flurry of introductions. I'm not sure I'll keep everyone's names straight, but I can't stop a grin from consuming my face. It's amazing, being swallowed alive by the love of family and friends, gathered to celebrate.

"They'll be here any minute!" Kate shouts, and the room falls quiet, except for the faint music playing over the speakers. "Positions."

Arthur comes beside Kate, Grant takes Quinn's hand, and Claude wraps his arm around Gwen's shoulders, pulling her to his side. These people—couples I admired and supported, standing as a unified front of strength and love—leave me speechless and a bit emotional. I clear my throat and look at the floor, willing myself to keep it together. This isn't about me or my miraculous return. I embrace this for the gift it is.

My found family reunited once more. Nothing could make me happier.

A warm hand takes mine. I look up to find Jessica beside me. Her fingers interlace with mine. I hold her deep blue gaze, and the air rushes from my lungs. This is what I'm here for. This is what I need.

Her.

That smile shatters my last thread of resolve.

"Jessica," I whisper. "I—"

The door swings open, and a chorused shout echoes through the bar. "Surprise! Happy birthday, Marcy!"

Jessica turns to greet her aunt, pulling me with her. My heart pounds in my chest at the gesture. She's claiming me. Showing them all there's something here. It gives me hope. A small spark. A tiny victory worth savoring.

Maybe she wants more. Wants me.

Marcy wraps me in a tight hug and showers my face with kisses. I'm pretty sure I have mauve lipstick all over my face, but I don't care. It feels great to be welcomed with open arms.

I shake Rob's hand, and he winks knowingly when Jessica comes beside me and rests her hand on my arm.

It's only natural when I wrap my arm around her waist, draw her to my side, and kiss her head.

Jessica spins and our eyes lock. She chuckles and shakes her head.

"What? You can't tell me they don't already know." I laugh.

She squeezes my hand. "You're right, but now we're the talk of the party."

I scan the crowd. No one's even looking at us. "I doubt that."

"The night is still young." Jessica cups my face in her hands and kisses me soundly.

With a groan, I pull her close and ensure she's thoroughly kissed. When we break apart, there's a smattering of applause in the background.

"Mission accomplished," she says with a breathy laugh.

Ignoring a pressing desire to take her home, party be damned, I pull away. "Come on. Let's mingle."

She drags me through the crowd, and Jackie hands us each a drink.

The envelope burns a hole in my chest, next to my thundering heart. I hope I don't fuck this up.

CHAPTER TWENTY-TWO
JESSICA

Is this as good as it gets?

The thought strikes me as Cyril holds me close, swaying to the music. I balked at first when he took my hand and pulled me to him, but Bryan Adams's tantalizing lyrics are enough to make any hard-hearted girl swoon. I can still remember the first time I heard this song, long before I watched *Robin Hood: Prince of Thieves*.

Tonight, the lyrics hit differently. The tempo lulls me into a peace I haven't felt in years…but that could just be Cyril's presence. Heat builds between us with every rocking sway. I inhale deeply, memorizing the scent of spicy aftershave mixed with his unique aroma.

The clock on the wall reads eight fifteen. Everyone over the age of fifty has departed along with those with children. There are only a handful of us lingering at the Black Penny. Jaqueline hangs out behind the bar, indulging us because we're family, and a reunion like this doesn't happen often.

In the chaos, I forgot to ask her about the progress of her divorce. I can always text her later. Tonight isn't for that conversation.

Cyril's hand tightens on my hip.

I glance up at him, only to find him staring off into space.

"Penny for your thoughts?" I ask, curiosity nibbling at my conscience.

He startles and meets my gaze. "Just thinking."

"What about?"

"You." His dimpled smile makes my insides flip.

"What about me?"

He inhales, like he's bracing to go underwater. When he exhales, it *whooshes* out of him in a rush. "I was thinking, I like this…us."

"Me too." I link my fingers together behind his neck, drawing him closer. "I can't believe it's only been a week since you showed up in my shop."

"Feels like a lifetime." His confession resonates deep inside me, a long-forgotten melody.

"It does." My heart flutters as he shifts his grip, his fingers trailing over my sides.

"I'm sorry if it's been a lot of change in a short period of time." He licks his lips, and the movement leaves me distracted with wicked thoughts. "I never meant to come in and mess everything up."

"Sometimes, change is a good thing, although it might not feel like it at the time. You didn't mess anything up."

"You said I did."

"I said a lot of things those first few days." Regret fills me. "I'm sorry about that. It wasn't very helpful. I should have been more understanding of your situation."

"You don't have to apologize. I understand. If I were in your position, I'd have been pissed off too."

A laugh escapes me, lightening the tension. "Still, it couldn't have been easy, dropping four decades into the future without knowing what the hell was going on."

"It wasn't." He spins me with a little flourish. "But I was lucky. I found you."

"When you found me, I wasn't very nice or helpful. How is that lucky?"

"It was exactly what I needed at that moment. So thank you."

My face warms under his scrutiny. I lean my head against his shoulder as the song changes to REO Speedwagon's "Keep on Lovin' You." Mom always called these songs *classic rock* when we were kids. I didn't understand why until I was older. Until I learned the truth of her and Dad's first meeting.

Now I'm living my own surreal whirlwind romance, just like Mom and Dad did. I should be terrified of what this means, but there's no trace of hesitation or fear in my brain.

I close my eyes. This is comfortable. Safe. *Home.*

My final reservation leaves, and I embrace this for what it is. A miracle. Fate. Destiny.

"I love you, Jessica."

The soft words drift over me, a warm blanket settling around my shoulders. Then they take root in my mind.

"What did you say?" I pull back without breaking his hold.

"I love you." He braces like he's unsure of how I'll react.

A week ago, I would have called him crazy, but tonight, right now…his words unlock nothing but certainty.

I cling tighter to him, and his apprehension softens.

"I love you too."

"Really?" Joy blooms across his features, making him look ten years younger. "You sure?"

"Even though events of the past week make no sense, and your presence in this decade defies the laws of time and space, I've never been more sure of anything in my life."

He crushes me against him and kisses me. The taste of him ignites my ever present hunger. I'm tempted to cross Jackie and climb on top of him right here in the middle of her bar. But I manage to contain my desire, salvaging my relationship with the friend eyeing us suspiciously from behind the counter.

When he breaks the kiss, we cling to each other in a desperate attempt to regain our bearings. He presses a gentle kiss to my forehead before stepping away.

"Let's play darts."

I shake myself. The haze of lust slowly recedes, and I stare at him. "Darts?"

"Yeah. Do you know how to play?"

"Of course," I scoff.

"Then let's play." He moves to the rear of the bar where a dartboard hangs on the wall.

"What do I get if I win?" I ask, grabbing the darts.

"So confident." He laughs. "One of the reasons I love you. Set the terms."

"The garage."

His brow rises. "What about it?"

"If you win, it's yours. If I win, it's mine."

He rubs his jaw and groans.

"Too rich for your blood?" I tease. It's not like I'll hold him to these terms, but I'm curious. What will he do?

"Not at all." He takes off his jacket and drapes it over a chair. "I just don't want to upset you when I take it from you."

"Now who's being cocky?" I laugh and roll up my sleeves.

"Fine. It's a bet." He extends his hand; I shake it.

A thrill rolls through me at the impending challenge. I have the upper hand. When I was in college, I was unbeatable at darts. There's no way Cyril knows this. No way in hell.

He offers me the floor first. I throw. Bullseye. Fifteen. Ten.

Cyril nods before taking his turn. Six. Twenty. Bullseye.

"Jackie, keep score for us," I shout as Cyril tries to use the scorekeeper. "I want to make sure this is legit."

"You got it." Jackie rounds the bar and sits off to the side with a pad and pen.

Back and forth we go. By the third round, we've gathered a small crowd. Most of them cheer for me, but there are a few for Cyril. Jackie keeps score, meticulously counting and writing down every point.

The last round begins, and Cyril makes his final throws. It's close. So close.

Chatter flows through the crowd, and the noise hums in my head.

"Last chance, Jess." Jackie's announcement hushes the crowd. "Cyril's up by fifteen. One bullseye and you win."

I can't blow this.

Or can I?

Does it matter?

Cyril loves me. Would he really take my dream when he knows how much it means to me?

I take a deep breath and throw.

Bullseye.

Holy shit! I did it.

The crowd erupts into applause around us. I'm barraged with congratulations and celebratory hugs. By the time they all disperse, I'm drunk with relief.

Cyril closes the gap between us. "Good game." He pulls me into a hug. "The garage is yours."

I bury my face in his shoulder. "It doesn't matter. It's just a game."

He draws back and reaches for his jacket. "No. A deal's a deal."

"I…"

My voice trails off when he reaches into his pocket and pulls out an envelope. He hands it to me.

"What's this?"

"Open it." He bites his lower lip, letting it slide between his teeth.

I open the barely sealed envelope and pull out the papers inside. Skimming the contents, I freeze.

Deed. Jessica Maxwell.

Wait. It can't be.

"What is this?"

"The deed to the building." Cyril grins, shoving his hands in his pockets.

"How did you convince Dad to…"

My eyes widen when the realization strikes me. "Dad never owned the building, did he?" I stumble back and collapse into a chair.

Cyril inclines his head. "Technically, he did, but I was on the deed too."

"So all this time, *you* were the owner of Cyril's Garage?" Disbelief rips through me.

"That's what Arthur tells me." He takes the seat beside me. "He bought the building with the intent to give it to me after I got the business established. When I disappeared, he held onto it, always making sure my name was on the deed."

A sob chokes me as I stare at the paper in my hand. "Then why are you giving me this?"

"The garage wouldn't be what it is today without you." He takes my free hand. "It was your blood, sweat, and tears that made the garage so successful. I could never take that accomplishment away from you."

Tears slide down my face, and I swipe them away with the back of my hand, careful not to get the paper wet. He understands. My tears flow harder at the realization.

Cyril takes the deed and sets it aside. Then he gathers me, pulling me into a firm embrace. I wrap my arms around his chest. My soft sobs are lost in the fabric of his shirt and the warm skin beneath it. When I finally compose myself, I step back, just enough to face him.

"Thank you." They're the only words I can manage. Everything else is lost.

"Don't thank me." Those dimples flash again. "I fully intend to take advantage of the next six months. There's no way in hell I'm letting you go now."

My brows furrow. "Six months?"

"Our agreement. A partnership for six months. To see what happens between us. Remember?"

Heat radiates through me at the reminder. "Yeah."

His soft kiss leaves me wanting more.

"Let's go home and celebrate." The whispered words ignite an inferno deep inside me.

I nod, and we say our goodbyes. I let him drive home, not trusting myself behind the wheel. When I get him alone, all bets are off.

He's mine. It thrills me more than my name on the deed in my pocket.

CHAPTER TWENTY-THREE
CYRIL

Her face was priceless.

The moment she opened the envelope and recognized her name on the deed, my heart stopped beating. I was afraid I'd overplayed my hand.

When I answered Arthur's phone call on Christmas morning, I told him I didn't want the shop and asked him to put the deed in her name. Two days of patience led me to the perfect setup. Our little game of darts set the stage. It was always my intention to give her the shop, the business, the whole shebang.

It takes all my effort to focus on the road and not the woman in the passenger seat. I make a right, and the glow of the shop's sign comes into view.

The garage was hers, regardless of her win. It was never mine, even if Arthur had my name on the paperwork. It wasn't *my* effort, *my* life poured into making the business a success. Jessica did that. And her happiness is all that matters. Period.

She reaches over and presses the garage opener clipped to the sun visor. The sweet, heady scent of her soap weaves into my brain, causing a short circuit. My grip tightens on the steering wheel.

I pull into the garage and turn off the ignition. The door lowers behind us.

When I get out of the car, I take in the shop around us. Her influence is everywhere, from the decorative tin images along the upper part of the walls to the meticulous organization of the tools. Jessica deserves this. All of it.

If that means I take orders from her as we move forward, so be it. I'd rather run the business with her than have her fear the fate of her investment. To me, it's a double win. She gets the security of knowing it's hers to do with as she pleases while knowing I value her hard work and determination.

This place doesn't need me. It needs *her*. She's the lifeblood. The reason for its existence.

"You coming?" she asks from the doorway to the upstairs apartment.

"Yeah." I tap the front end of the Swinger as I walk by, like a good luck charm, and turn off the lights when I reach the door.

She's at the top of the stairs when I finally catch up to her. "Key?" Her hand sits palm up.

I lift her hand to my lips and press a kiss to her palm. She bites her lip, eyes darkening at the simple action. I place the keys in her hand.

Jessica fumbles with the lock for a few seconds until it finally clicks open. The moment we're inside, she spins around and pins me against the wall beside the door. Her hands hold firm against my chest. Her eyes the color of a midday summer storm.

"Before this goes any further, I need to know something." Her husky voice creates goosebumps along my skin.

"What's that?"

"Did you throw the game?"

I laugh. "What?"

"Did you let me win at darts?"

"Do you think I'm capable of that?" I study her face closely, noting the way her lip twitches and her nostrils flare when she's worked up. It's fucking adorable.

"I don't know what you're capable of, Cyril."

"You sure about that?" I tease my fingers under the hem of her shirt, finding her warm soft skin, stroking gently.

"Just tell me the truth."

"Why does it matter?" My fingers drift higher until they brush the delicate curve of her breast. I want my mouth there, but she won't relent. Not until she has her answer.

"You had the deed before we played, but there's no way you knew I could win." She steps closer, licking her lips and pushing her body into mine. "You threw the game so you could give me that deed."

Every delicious curve molds against me, and I'm desperate to be inside her. "If I tell you the truth, will you let me fuck you?"

"You're getting fucked either way."

A smirk steals onto her full lips. I imagine them wrapped around my cock like Christmas morning and groan.

"You're not giving me any incentive, love."

"That wasn't my intention." She trails her hand over my stomach and cups my erection through the material pulled tight over it.

"You're killing me."

"Did you throw the game?" She squeezes gently, increasing the pressure with each word.

"No." I gasp, unable to take it any longer. "I didn't throw the game."

My body nearly gives out when she releases her hold and steps back.

With a sultry glance over her shoulder, she pulls off her jacket and ventures into the living room, where she drops it to the floor. Then she pulls off her glittery top followed by her black lace bra. When they hit the floor, I push away from the wall and stumble after her.

My clothes follow, joining hers on the floor in a trail to the couch.

We're both naked, standing in the middle of the living room. I wrap my arms around her waist and pull her against me. My hand slides between her thighs.

"Shit. You're so wet."

She nods.

"For me?" I nip at her shoulder.

"Yes." Her gasp breaks on a moan when I bite harder and slide my fingers inside her.

"Can I play with your pussy?"

"Why does that sound hot when you say it?"

"Is that a yes?"

"Yes." She spins and pushes me down to the sofa.

I grab her wrist and pull her across my lap.

"Alexa, play the Cars." I grin at Jessica's startled reaction.

"Moving In Stereo" drifts through the speakers.

"How did you…?"

"Shh." Her question dissipates when I part her thighs and stroke along her seam. "The only words I want to hear from your lips right now are *yes*, *please*, and *more*."

"Confident, are you?"

I press my thumb against her clit. She bucks her hips, arching her back.

"Damn it, Cyril." Her moan echoes through the room, harmonizing with the music.

With two fingers, I delve deep while my thumb works its magic. She writhes beneath my hand, and I use the other to gently squeeze her nipple. Her body hums as I stroke her higher and higher. Her desperation for release has my cock twitching, wanting to be included.

Jessica's cries echo off the walls when she comes. It hits her hard and fast, and I wring every last shuddering wave of pleasure from her body before I relent.

I gather her in my arms, cradle her to my chest. Her body trembles against me, still sensitive from her orgasm. After a few moments, she shifts to straddle my thighs. Her slick pussy rubs against my cock.

My body tenses as she slides down my hard length. I take several deep breaths once she's taken all of me. It's like Christmas Eve, when we fucked in the car. Only this time, there's no limit in any capacity. No physical restraints, no emotional barriers.

It's just us. Partners. Lovers. Friends. Nothing could be more perfect.

"Mine." I tighten my grip on her hips.

"Mine." She links her arms around my neck.

My restraint snaps, and I thrust up into her. She meets my motion with her own, rocking her hips in time with the music as the song switches to "Just What I Needed."

Delirious with want for her, I lose myself in the moment, taking every stroke and returning it with fervor. She clings to me and uses my shoulders as leverage to drive me deeper.

Her head tips back, her hair trailing down her spine. I wrap my hand in her curls, tighten the hair around my fist, and pull. She hisses and swears, but her pussy pulses around me as another orgasm builds.

"That's it, baby." I push her closer, letting her grind her hips into mine. The friction builds, and she flutters around my cock. Close. So damn close.

I kiss her hard, swallow her panting moans. My own release builds, but I want her there, spilling over the edge when I come.

She rips free and digs her nails into my shoulders when her climax finally hits. Her pace slows with the force of it, draining her.

I push her down onto the couch and fuck her into the cushions. Her pleasure-dazed eyes stare up at me, her lips parted. With every thrust, she grins wider, urging me on with soft moans, digging her nails into my ass.

When I come, she looks happy. A woman utterly sated with pleasure.

"Stay here." I climb off the couch and retreat to the bathroom. When I return with a warm cloth, I clean her, then myself before rejoining her on the couch. She snuggles against me, pulling a blanket over us.

"Shall we go to bed?" Her fingertips drift over my bare chest.

"I was hoping we could sit like this for a little while." I kiss her forehead.

"Okay." She turns her head. "Alexa, turn off music."

The music stops, and she reaches for the remote.

"What are you doing?"

"Turning something on." She presses the power button and finds the Disney app.

"Like what?"

"You'll see." Jessica scans through the selections until a title pops up on the screen.

"*The Force Awakens?*"

"Yeah."

I laugh. "I thought you didn't like *Star Wars?*"

"No, I said I've never *seen Star Wars*. There's a difference." She hits play.

"Maybe we should start with *A New Hope*."

"It doesn't matter. I'm sure you'll make me watch all of them multiple times."

I wrap my arm around her and pull her closer. "Have I told you before how much I love you?"

"Yes, but tell me again. It's been a while."

"I love you." The words spill out through laughter.

"Good, because I love you too." She props her feet on my legs beneath the blanket.

The movie starts, and I'm sucked into the story.

Later that night, as we're lying in bed, amid thoughts of betrayal and red light sabers, dreams of us take root in my mind. Possibilities and hope. The cogs click into place.

Being here, now, won't be easy, but I'll adapt and learn, especially with Jessica beside me. When she's ready, I'll ask the question slowly consuming my mind.

I'm not in a rush. I have a whole life ahead of me. Having Jessica in it will be the gilded trim on the sports car. She needs this time as much as I do to figure out what she wants.

I'm a patient man. I can wait. Victory will be that much sweeter.

Until then, I'm content. Truly.

CHAPTER TWENTY-FOUR
JESSICA

Six Months Later

I pull up to the curb down the street from Mom and Dad's brownstone, basking in relief at finding some prime parking, and turn off the ignition.

Cyril casts a dimpled grin in my direction before getting out of the car.

"What?" I ask, climbing out of the driver's seat.

"Nothing." He closes the door and turns away from me.

The summer sunshine beams down, and I let it soak into my skin. I can't believe it's been six months since I first brought him here. A total stranger who upended my life for the better.

Since we joined forces, Cyril's Car Services has expanded to three locations across five boroughs, with plans for three more in the works. Between the two of us, we've made a name for the shop. His old-school ideas mixed with my new school technology. We rebranded Cyril's and cultivated a whole new clientele.

The two of us make a banging team.

Pun intended.

He takes my arm and nudges me. "What are you laughing about?"

"Nothing." I throw his response back in his face, and he scoffs. "Hey, what's good for the goose is good for the gander."

"Smart-ass."

We climb the stairs and knock before entering the house. My siblings have already arrived with their children. The younger ones gather around Cyril, begging him to play with them in the garden. He kisses my cheek and bounds behind them, heading for the narrow green space my parents have cultivated in the heart of the city.

"There you are." Mom wipes her hands on her apron when I enter the kitchen. She searches the hallway behind me when I come in alone. "Where's Cyril?"

"The kids dragged him to the backyard."

"Dad's out there. He'll make sure they behave." My sister winks and finishes prepping the sandwiches.

"So." Mom's voice lowers. "When are you two going to make it official?"

"Mom, you can't rush these things." I roll my eyes.

I love Cyril dearly, and I can't imagine my life without him. We've got a good thing going. Our partnership is blossoming, and so is our sex life. I'm content with what we have. It's comfortable. No pressure. Well, except from Mom and Dad, who claim they're not getting any younger. Like it really impacts them. Cyril and I are happy together, and that's fine with me. For now.

Mom huffs and tries to lift the tray of sandwiches.

"Let me get it." I shoo her away and pick up the over-burdened tray. "You shouldn't be carrying this heavy stuff anymore. Doctor's orders."

"As if." Mom waves her hand dismissively, but she leads the way, letting me carry the food to the backyard.

"Need help?" Cyril stands when I step onto the back patio.

"Sure." I gesture toward Mom with my elbow.

Ever the gentleman, he takes her arm and leads her to a chair beside Dad. I set the tray on the table. He follows me to the kitchen to help carry out the last of the food.

"I forgot the wine. It's in the car."

"I'll get it." Cyril offers, holding out his hand for the key.

"Thanks, babe." I kiss his cheek before he darts back inside.

"So when's the wedding?" Dad asks with a smirk.

"Why's everyone in such a hurry?"

"What? I can't want to see my daughter happily married before I die?" he grumbles.

"You're not going to die for another twenty years. At least. Hush." I make him a plate with two sandwiches.

The kids run around the small open space behind us. Their parents have set up a picnic table and chairs off to the side, careful of the renegade soccer ball.

It's perfect. I couldn't ask for a better summer day. Relaxing with my family, soaking up the sun. Cyril reappears in the doorway with a bottle of wine. My heart flutters when he meets my gaze and smiles.

Yup, it's perfect.

"Here's the wine." He sets it on the table in front of my parents.

"Keys?" I ask, holding out my hand. "I don't want to lose them."

Cyril turns to hand them to me but they fall to the grass. "Whoops." He drops down and picks them up.

But he doesn't stand.

He's on one knee.

Gasps echo around me, but I can't hear anything. I can't see anything but the man before me, kneeling like a knight in shining armor, my key ring dangling from his fingertips.

Beside it is a ring with a diamond glimmering in the sunlight.

"Jessica, when I showed up at the shop that morning, I didn't know what to expect from the future." He takes a deep breath. "But the moment I saw you working on that 1974 Swinger, I knew you were the woman for me."

Laughter bubbles around us, but I stay focused on him. My lip trembles.

"I'm sorry I caused you so much trouble," he continues. "It wasn't my intention. I didn't have a friend in the world…at least not one under seventy." More laughter. "You taught me how to survive modern technology. I showed you the value of being old school."

My heart beats wildly against my ribs, and joy chokes me.

"We make a fantastic team, and I don't want anyone else by my side. Will you be my wife? My partner for life?"

"That's so corny." I laugh, even though tears fill my eyes. "But it's so you."

"Is that a yes?" Hope glimmers in his eyes.

"Yes," I say with a laugh. "Of course it's a yes."

Cheers erupt around us. Cyril climbs to his feet and pulls me into his arms.

When he kisses me, the chaos fades to background noise. He pulls back and brushes a stray curl from my face.

Never in a million years would I have imagined this moment. This man. The universe knew what it was doing when it plucked him from the past and dropped him in my lap. I didn't appreciate it at the time, but I do now.

He is exactly what I need in my life.

"I love you."

"Love you too." I squeeze him tight.

"Finally! Took you long enough." Dad's voice rises over the noise, cutting through our tender moment. "Can we eat now?"

Cyril and I laugh.

He's right though. It's about damn time.

CHAPTER TWENTY-FIVE
CYRIL

"Are you sure you don't want to go somewhere fancy to celebrate?" I ask, pushing open the door to the Black Penny.

"What's wrong with the Penny?" Jessica scoffs and pushes past me.

"Nothing."

We step inside, and the door closes behind me. The familiar sights and smells surround me, both from the eighties and last December when I challenged her to darts for the deed to the garage.

"This is a great place to celebrate our engagement."

Jessica shoots me a look and shakes her head. "Come on." She tugs my hand, pulling me deeper into the bar.

There's a crowd. Typical for a Friday night, but not as busy as I've seen it. We've made the Penny one of our weekly dates—I buy her a few drinks, she challenges me to darts. Then we go home and fuck. It's a win-win all around.

"Hey!" Jackie calls from behind the bar. She whispers something to the other bartender before coming out to join us. "Congrats."

"Word travels fast," I mutter as she pulls me into a hug.

"You really think my dad wouldn't call his friends and tell them the good news?" Jessica laughs and hugs Jackie.

"He called my dad right after you left. Then Dad called me." Jackie shrugs. "I guess I'm glad he didn't call everyone to tell them when my divorce was finalized."

"Congrats!" Jessica hugs her again. "He was a dick. You're better off without him."

"I am." Jackie laughs and lowers her voice. "I just don't need it broadcast across the city. I have enough problems with men hitting on me without them knowing I'm single again."

"Not interested in trying for round two?" I ask, pulling Jessica close and resting my hand on her hip.

"No. Abso-fucking-lutely not." She grins. "I've got enough problems to deal with running this place. This girl is off the market."

"Well, I'm happy for you. You deserve to take some time for yourself," Jessica says.

"Why don't you guys have a seat? I'll send a waitress over." Jackie gestures to the bar. "I gotta get back to work."

"Thanks." I lead Jessica to a booth along the far wall.

We settle onto the pleather bench and pick up the menus, even though we know exactly what we want.

"The usual?" Jessica asks.

"Yup." I push aside the menu and scan the bar. "Good crowd tonight."

"Mm-hmm."

"He's back," I say, my voice low.

"No way." Jessica's head snaps up from the menu. She spies the man in question. "He's in the same spot as last week?"

"Yeah. The far end of the bar. Back against the wall."

"Who is he?"

"I don't have a clue. Never met the guy."

"What's he doing here all the time?"

I study the mysterious man, watching his movements for a few moments. He takes a drink. Glances at his phone. Then looks up, his gaze following someone behind the bar.

Jackie.

"Shit."

"What?" Jessica claws at my hand. "Don't leave me in suspense."

"He's watching Jackie."

"Should we tell her?"

Jackie's attention fixes on the man in question. She puts a hand on her hip and scowls.

"Nope. She's already aware of it."

"What do you think he wants?"

I'm too far away to accurately read his expression, but I've been around long enough to know when someone's thirsty…and the drink in their hand isn't what they want.

Mindy, our waitress, arrives and takes our order. When she leaves, we gravitate toward the drama brewing at the bar. Jackie approaches the man and takes his empty glass.

Shit, I wish I could hear what they were saying, but there's too much commotion to even try to read their lips.

When our drinks arrive, we give up. I make a mental note to ask Jackie about it later.

I lift my glass in salute. "To us. Partners for life."

"Cheers." She clinks her glass against mine and takes a sip.

"Movie tonight?" I ask, settling back against the booth.

She gives me a look that says, *Really?*

"What? I have years of catching up to do."

"Fine." Jessica sets her glass down. "But we're not watching *Star Wars* again."

"You're no fun."

"There are hundreds of other movies to watch."

"Fine." I tap my fingers on the table.

Her eyes brighten. "I know. We'll watch *Willow.* You haven't seen it yet."

"What's *Willow?* Sounds sappy."

She laughs, and the sound makes my whole body vibrate with need.

"Trust me. You'll love it."

"Sounds like there's something in this for you?"

A wicked smile curves her lips. "There is." She sighs. "Madmartigan."

"It's a hot guy, isn't it?"

Her laughter breaks free, and she nods.

"Am I not hot enough?" I pat my chest and run my hands over my T-shirt.

Jessica bites her lip. "You're smoking hot, babe."

"You're teasing me?"

She nods again. "You make it so easy."

I fold my arms across my chest and grumble. "Who plays this Madmartigan?"

"Val Kilmer."

"I take it back. He's hot."

Jessica reaches across the table and takes my hand. "I love you."

"I love you too." I look at the waitress approaching with our food. "Think we can get it to go?"

"No. Let's enjoy our meal." She releases my hand and winks. "You can have dessert later."

I pick up a French fry and shove it in my mouth. "Tease."

She blows a kiss to me. "You love it."

You're goddamn right I do.

Whispering a prayer of thanks, I drink her in. There's nowhere I'd rather be.

THE END

OTHER BOOKS BY KIRSTEN S. BLACKETER

CRAVING 1985 SERIES
When I Found You
Can't Fight This Feeling
She Gives Love a Bad Name
Owner of a Lonely Heart
Just What I Needed

HISTORICAL
An Irresistible Shadow
A Shadow's Kiss
Mississippi Moonshine
Deceiving the Earl
Jewel of Winter
At Winter's Demand
Under Winter's Control
Seducing Winter's Gentleman
Stealing the Widow's Heart
Seduction on the Alpine Express
Temptation on the Alpine Express

CONTEMPORARY
A Lockdown Love Affair
A Holiday Love Affair
Mistletoe and Mistakes
Confessions of a Fangirl
Confessions of a Gamer Girl
Confessions of a Glamour Girl
The Flight Before Christmas

FANTASY/FAIRYTALE
Curse of the Huntsman's Jewel
The Huntsman's Revenge

PIRATES AND PERSUASION
Queen Takes Hook

ABOUT THE AUTHOR

Kirsten S. Blacketer is a multi-published indie author of both historical and contemporary romance. When she's not writing, she homeschools her two children and enjoys time with her family. In those moments of freedom, she devours romance novels while sipping a glass of wine. Age has only shown her that writing villains can be just as fun as heroes. Her next life goals are to write a New York Times Bestseller and one day have Adam Driver play a starring role in a film version of one of her books. A girl can dream, right?

Read more at **http://kirstensblacketer.com.**

ALSO WRITES AS JEN BRADLEE